At the Time of the P
Wars: Aftermath©

Truth is stranger than fiction, but it is because Fiction is obliged to stick to possibilities: Truth isn't.

Mark Twain. *Following the Equator: A Journey Around the World*

There are alternative facts.

Kellyanne Conway Advisor to President D. J. Trump. *Meet the Press* January 22, 2017.

Foreword March 2021

This work was originally published in 2006 under the title *Towards New Eden: Aftermath.* I have changed the title because of some confusion about this being a religious work – which it is not.

Before starting to write the first book in 2002, I spent several years researching a range of socio-economic, political, environmental and religious trends.

This is the 1st edition under this title. The work is hopefully, improved by removing any remaining grammatical and typographical errors.

There are no changes to the original plot or characters.

The prequel *At the Time of the Presidents' Wars: Towards New Eden* and the sequel *At the Time of the Presidents' Wars: Between Hell and High Water* are available on Amazon and Kindle.

Chapter I

WashingtonWall

22.48 UTC March 18th

Lopez had insisted in holding the meeting in the old Oval Office, despite continued concerns about a second attack. The constant trickle of news revealed that, whilst the Christians had failed in their assumed primary objectives, breaches in Wall sections and other damage had caused several thousand more civilian and military fatalities than first reported. However, the damage to strategic military facilities had been minimal and the White House itself was still functioning despite the damage.

For the umpteenth time that evening he looked at the picture of his family on the desk in front of him, and then turned again to the small pile of dispatches. Inevitably there was the message from Vice President Howard, nestling in the safety of California, asking of Lopez's well-being and offering to assume the Presidency whilst Lopez mourned the loss of his family. *'Give him the Presidency and I'll never see it again,'* Lopez mulled to himself , whilst struggling to decide what level of desperation had forced him to embrace such a despicable individual as running-mate. Equally inevitably, there was a scattering of messages from some of the South American states. Lopez was intrigued by the speed with which the news had spread and wondered if, or when, he would hear from elsewhere.

What had attracted his attention was a curt message from Premier Yang-Laval which read simply: '*The Government of Free Canada communicates its condolences on both your personal and public losses. I have ordered our armed forces to cooperate with you in locating and destroying the perpetrators.*'

What do the Canadians have Andy? And I trust your family is well? Lopez asked as soon as Admiral Cutler had taken his place at the table.

My family is safe thank you Mr. President. As for the Canadians, may I ask why are you asking? And you mean naval capability? If not, perhaps we should wait for…

No, naval Intel is what I'm after. Can they help us in a meaningful way to track down and destroy Smith?

Cutler sat back in his seat and gazed thoughtfully at a new crack in the ceiling for a full minute before replying. *They have a few good ships Mr. President. Like us, they were weakened by both religious and secessionist wars, but they appear to have come through better. Didn't have as many religious crazies from what we understand, but you need to talk to one of the intelligence agencies rather than me about that. What I can tell you is that they may be able to help a*

bit - and if they are being friendly, then I would take the offer. We need all the help we can get.
Anderson's arrival concluded the conversation. This was a decision Lopez was going to make on his own, and later that night he made a discrete call to Montreal on the secure line.

Nuova Lisboa

09.18 UTC March 20th

There was something about the new capital of the Portuguese province which was simultaneously exhilarating and frustrating. There had been insufficient money or forward planning to create a Wall to protect the original city, so large areas near the seafront had been abandoned. However, huge sums had been expended in saving culturally symbolic structures such as the Belem Tower which had been dismantled and then carefully re-built on high land overlooking the old capital. Henry understood the place was called Bairro Alto. The incongruity had been completed by constructing a regional airbase immediately adjacent to the tower, thereby adding a collection of medieval monuments to the hazards of take-off and landing.
Not that Henry was complaining. Since their arrival his time had been spent either sunbathing or exploring the historical monuments with Marie-Claire. Both activities were regardless of Brown's

innuendoes that the relationship was becoming a tad too close and that *Mrs. Henry might not approve.* Now it was another gorgeous morning, and the plan had been to take a bus down to a local beach and wait until further orders came through.

That had been the plan, but the night had been marked by a sudden burst of noisy activity. This morning there was both an air of tension and the absence of his potential swimming partner. He considered the latter a great shame given the time and energy he had expended trying to find a pair of fitting swimming trunks. Before leaving London he had literally swept an old, hard book from the shelf on the way out of the door and jammed it into his case. And so it was he found himself sitting on a rickety wooden bench and on page eight of one of Rachel's eighteenth century romances. Suddenly, intuitively, he felt the easy times were about to finish as he watched a vehicle ploughing a furrow of dust from the base entrance directly towards where he was sitting. Though they had repeatedly swept for bugs, neither he nor Brown had been able to decide exactly how the Europeans always seemed to know where they were, and there was now a tacit agreement that this was an irrelevance given the apparent freedom they were granted. Henry's suspicions were justified when the cross-country

swung to a halt showering him in a fine cloud of dust.
Mr. La Fontaine? enquired the Eurocorp sergeant leaning out of the window. Without waiting for confirmation he continued *You are required immediately at the briefing place. And your lady friend. You know where she is?* and Henry detected the slightest hint of a smile as though to say *'Who is she sleeping with this morning?'* He had no answer to the question, and no sooner had he clambered into the vehicle than it lurched forward, throwing him from side-to-side as the suspension struggled to cope with the potholed road. This time he was genuinely puzzled as to where Amanda had managed to find a fresh bed to pass the night. He had informed the sergeant that, to the best of his knowledge, Ms Brown was on the base, but the question was answered as they slewed into the main gate and he caught side of her distinctive ginger hair emerging from one of the detached houses reserved for senior officers. *Bloody sleeping her way up the ranks,* he muttered, causing his driver to give him a quizzical look. The Englishman must already have had too much sun.
They ground to a halt outside a new, brilliant-white, building with the same delicacy as they had set off. The brilliance of the white set Henry thinking briefly about new fashions in European military

camouflage before he found himself whisked into the building, down a wide cool corridor and then, to his surprise, to a podium in an auditorium crowded with military personnel.

There was a near tangible tension in the air. *What's up?* Henry enquired of one of the officers seated behind him, and almost immediately realised he had made another communications error. All of the military Henry had encountered knew at least a minimal, operation English and could generally shame both himself and Brown in their range of languages. However, this *what's up?* – whilst not on a par with Poo Bear – threatened to demand a reasonable explanation as the officer raised his eyes quizzically upwards. *The ceiling is up? Why do you ask this?* he replied with a strong accent suggesting he came from one of the Slavic contingents. Henry was saved from having to try and explain the meaning of his informal question by the room standing to attention as one. A five star general had entered, followed by Amanda who shot another of her coquettish glances at Henry. *'Slept with the jackpot this time,'* he found himself thinking. This time he managed to keep the thought to himself. The two came directly to the podium and, in perfect English, the assembled group was told to be seated.

What followed left Henry stunned. The assembly was informed in cool, strategic terms of news from the Federal American government that a terrorist attack had been launched on the national capital and that the perpetrators, in their tens of thousands, were believed to be approaching Europe in heavily armed warships with nuclear and other mass-destruction capabilities. It was a brief exposition of the facts, but through it Henry noted that Amanda was frequently looking at him in a manner he could not quite fathom. Initially, he thought it was a means to stress her latest conquest. Henry had yet to decide whether these represented personal, biological whims or whether she had a less than cunning strategy to wheedle information from each of her 'victims' as Henry liked to think of them. There was also something inherently animal in their own relationship, and the longer he was away from London the greater

His urge was to try his luck bedding either Amanda or Marie-Claire. Of the two, Marie-Claire represented something less threatening despite her latent ability to put Henry in a hospital bed – or worse- within seconds. Finally, to his consternation it dawned on him that Amanda's signals had nothing to do with her personal intent and everything to do with the fact that he was THE expert on Smith, and the name was being used with increasing frequency by the officer briefing the hall, and then the word *'expert'* started to pepper the sentences. He knew that within seconds the words *'expert'* and *'La Fontaine'* would be co-joined and had started to formulate a semi-reasonable hypothesis to explain Smith's behaviour when silence feel and his neighbour prodded Henry into an awareness that several hundred eyes were trained on him.

The next twenty minutes were less than comfortable. True, he had spent hours discussing world problems with Smith over late-night drinks and strong early-morning coffee. True, he had even shared a room with the man for a few weeks. True, he had written his doctoral thesis on the rise of the Christian right in America and Smith's role. It was not, however, true to claim that he could predict Smith's future strategy with any certainty. It was this that the assembled military wanted.

Given his knowledge, the most likely explanation he could offer was that Smith had convinced himself that the American faithful should re-locate themselves in the traditional Holy Lands. The man had often spoken of his desire to re-establish a true religious state and had regularly praised the ultra-Orthodox elements in the old State of Israel. The likelihood was of a warm reception there was beyond Henry's knowledge, but he noticed several concerned glances between the senior staff when he raised the possibility. What he could say with certainty that the Smith he had known and studied abhorred both failure and rejection, and could prove highly dangerous if he failed to get his way. His best advice? To let him pass freely through European waters unless he demonstrated hostile intentions.

So no invasion of Spanish or Portuguese lands? someone finally asked. It was the question that all had been mulling over, but no one had vocalised.

I suppose he might consider some of the old religious sites as legitimate settlements, Henry conceded. *Perhaps places like .... what's the old pilgrim place in the north called?*

You mean Compostella? someone chipped in helpfully.

Yes, that's the name. He might consider that – but I don't believe it has the status to justify a voyage like this. Not amongst his people at least. Henry replied.

And why he leave many of his people behind? demanded a burly captain on the front row.

He left many of his people behind? Henry demanded, surprised at the news. *He paused, weighing the information carefully. Smith hates to lose face with people. If he has left followers behind I suspect it is because they believe they will do something useful or...* and he paused, weighing his words carefully. *Or because he, and they, believe something spectacular is going to happen and he wants witnesses. Smith believes that witnessing his success is witnessing the approval of God, so he must be planning something very big.*

Like Washington? The attack on that could av been big if they kill the Presidente, someone at the back of the room demanded.

Purrhaps Henry conceded reluctantly. *That might have been it, but that seems a little small if the reports are accurate. He could have attacked Washington without all the civilians he has with him. No, it is like he is taking them to a new place – a new sanctuary. He has always had an obsession with the creation of a New Eden, or a New Jerusalem, depending on his mood and whenever we discussed things he insisted that this could only be created after the purification of the old, sinful, order.* He stopped, hesitating as an idea came into his mind. *I'm rather thinking on my feet here, but I just wonder if he has the capacity and inclination to launch a nuclear attack on the eastern seaboard.* A startled murmur went round the room. *It's simple speculation, but such a scenario does seem to make some sense of the intelligence. It also explains why he's moved the remnant of his people west – somewhere safe so that he can collect them later.*

So are you saying that he's planning on occupying European territory while all this is happening? demanded an officer whose quality of English and weight of metal on his uniform indicated considerable importance. Not for the first time Henry found himself cursing himself for the lack of attention he had paid to military ranks and insignia.

Perhaps, he eventually replied, *but it will have to be a place of some importance –especially of religious importance. It might even have crossed his mind to try to join with one of the Israeli groups, but that could be fraught with complications given his own religious and political beliefs and their own situation.*

So, your best advice? demanded the same officer.

Henry found himself increasingly irritated by the perfunctory tone in the questioner's voice which indicated that he was unimpressed with the on-going analysis. He decided to counter-attack. *My best advice? Well, I've given you the parameters as I see them. I have studied Smith, not every religious site in this part of Europe. I suggest your intelligence people have a look at those options. But your intelligence seems very limited so my advice must be limited. I don't know, for example, what his land and air capabilities are. Can he move inland or is he stuck with his ships? That's the sort of information you have, and I haven't, so once we have more details we can look again at the likely scenarios. I'd be happy to help further at that stage.*

If Henry had felt embarrassed and corned by the unexpected calling of the meeting, he suddenly felt the tables turned. The air marshal – at least that was what Henry had finally guesstimated his rank to be- had paled and looked away in the face of what Henry realised had been a relatively sustained onslaught on his part. *'Perhaps I've over-done it,'* he thought to himself, and the realisation flooded back into his mind that he was far from home amongst people whose relationship with his own government was less than warm, and in a world in which accidents were increasingly common. *'Lost in flight on return to London,'* came into his mind as a suitable explanation for his potential demise, and then he realised that it was not his approach but his words which were the issue. Inadvertently, he had asked questions which were either of great concern to the top brass or which they had failed to consider. *That'll teach you to be pompous with me you fat bastard* he found himself thinking and then, seeing the shock on Amanda's face, realised that he had articulated the sentence sufficiently for the microphone to have carried it to the entire assembly.

Nuova Lisboa
12.27 UTC March 20th

Fucking brilliant, Amanda burbled yet again, slurping violently from a litre bottle of cheap, local white. *I've never seen anyone manage to upset so many important people, so quickly, in my entire fucking life.* She'd stopped giggling soon after the third mouthful as the enormity of Henry's faux pas dawned on her. *We'll be lucky if they don't just drop us into the sea you know. They didn't rate your intelligence brief so hot, and then you upset El Grasso, or however you call a fat pig in Portuguese.* They were sitting in the shade of a large olive tree on the most remote part of the base; it was a refuge to which they had fled immediately after the briefing ended, stopping only for Amanda to buy some wine from the military store.

It'd have helped if you'd given me some warning, Henry snarled, giving the near-empty bottle an anxious glance. He'd barely had a mouthful and now the prospect loomed of a dry afternoon or the near certain humiliation involved in walking back to the store. In the back of his mind their lurked the darker spectre of the limits of their usefulness having been passed, with whatever dangers that involved. *And do you really have to sleep your way through the entire bloody lot? If you spent a bit more time focused on what we're here for, I might have known what was about to happen and...*

The sentence was unfinished as he ducked to avoid the bottle sailing past his head, and smashing onto the parched earth beyond the cooling shadow of the tree. *Don't you fucking lectuuure me,* Amanda slurred. *I have my ways and you have your clever, bloody theories. Don't you relise….realise we were sent to complement each other you stupid bastard, you...*

Playing nicely mes enfants? But you are so rude with each other! Neither had notice Marie-Claire arrive, nor had they any notion of how long she had been standing, silently in the shade behind them. *But don't be so upset. The fat pig –an Italian not a Portuguese one you should know- was not so displeased with Henry. And he was very pleased with you Amanda,* she added with a giggle *so you are both ok. You both live to, what is the expression in English? You live to fight again?*

You live to fight another bloody day, Amanda volunteered. *So what's the big plan now that we know that we know next to nothing?*

The big Italian pig's plan is to spend lots of money and use lots of fuel trying to find your Mr. Smith. In four days he is sending three squadrons out to the two hundred kilometre mark, with very big distances between the balloons. We are going to....... to scur?

Scour? Henry volunteered. *So, he's planning on sweeping the Atlantic and...yes, waiting for a few days so that Smith's ships should be coming into range if they are coming this way.*

Exactly enry, Marie-Claire confirmed with a broad smile. *And if you are both good you can come riding with us. Your knowledge may still be useful if we meet these Americans, and...* She stopped mid- sentence as Amanda collapsed against the tree. *Your poor friend,* she cried in mock alarm. *You English always did drink too much with the heat. You must take good care of her, but be careful not to catch nothing you do not want! You understand?* and with a smile she turned on her heels leaving Henry to deal with Amanda's first bout of vomiting.

Chapter II
A Parting of the Ways?
31.9 degrees north, 32.9 degrees west
06.09 UTC March 28th

Each day since the abortive attack on WashingtonWall had been a source of growing anguish for Monroe. As a seasoned military officer, it wasn't the waste of good men and equipment that weighed on his mind as much as the futility –lives lost for Smith's ego. But that was as nothing compared to the growing realization that control of the fleet was slipping through his fingers into the hands of a man who seemed to show ever greater brutality and indifference to life with each passing day.

The second day after the attack was one that Monroe remembered most distinctly. Two of the yachts out of the eastern coast were spotted semi-submerged directly ahead of his squadron. They had already heard their distress calls several hours earlier and witnessed a growing trail of detritus thrown overboard in a desperate effort to stay afloat. Despite Monroe's protestations, Smith had ordered that there be no response to the distress calls. Later, claiming concerns about a potential submarine attack, he had ordered they sail directly on with no attempt at rescue, despite pleas from the stricken vessels. One woman had even raised her infant above her head as a symbol of desperation. Monroe's humanism called for mercy, but he had been publicly over-ridden by Smith. Their difference had taken place on Monroe's own bridge in a breach of all established conventions, and he had been obliged to stand, smarting with the humiliation, until a suitable excuse arose to transfer command to another officer. Later, Monroe had checked the manifests which showed that, short of a divine miracle, another 150 lives had been pointlessly lost.

Not that all his concerns were altruistic. The previous morning he had had woken to find a new detachment of guards – Presidential guards now- posted outside his cabin. Not that he could complain. It was, of course, a great honour to have the President's personal escort guarding him, but his concern lay in the question as to whether he was being guarded as admiral or as a potential prisoner – his instincts told him the latter. And then there was that damned, fresh-faced lieutenant. The name had always evaded him, but he was now an ever-present part of the President's entourage. Monroe had finally learned his name -Adams- through the simple, though embarrassing, expedient of asking another junior officer. He had promptly checked his details on the ship's computer and there appeared to be nothing special about Adams. It seemed he'd majored in geography with a thesis on something Monroe couldn't fully understand -something to do with tectonic history it seemed- before briefly becoming involved with oil exploration. Then, he'd joined the cause as an ordinary seamen and been promoted on the basis of ability and zeal. A good man to have in a fight it seemed, but what made him so special that he had been singled out by Smith? The next day a problem had developed with his cabin computer link, and he hadn't had time to go and read further about his background.

But Adams was always there. As the days had passed Monroe noted that he and Smith seemed to enter into ever more regular discussions and that a coterie of officers and other ranks seemed to be swelling around them. Finally, Monroe had found the courage to ask Smith directly about what appeared to be some form of planning exercise, and had been fobbed off with some general comments about improving communication across the fleet and that it was something with which Monroe need not concern himself. It appeared that whatever Smith was planning was below the dignity of the fleet's admiral, but not below that of the President himself. Not that all was bad. They had rendezvoused with the fleet as planned, and Smith had been thrown into a fit of ecstasy to learn that -with the exception of the hulks they had passed en route- all ships had emerged unscathed from the storms. The Lord himself also appeared to be favouring them initially, a steady wind from the west driving them along at a good 15 knots without engine power.

Wherever they were going, Smith appeared certain that they were now sailing with the Lord's blessing, and in his new warmth he had even invited Monroe to his cabin for what he suspected was an attempt at peace-making. But the conversation had been stilted and intermittent, and Smith had rapidly found an excuse to finish the meeting. So it was that, though nominally overall commander of the day-to-day running of the fleet, Monroe felt that his writ was both limited and that he was being excluded from something important. But what?

Now, the wind had fallen to no more than the slightest breeze, and Smith had entered yet another of his dark moods in which he questioned why the Lord was showing him less favour. He argued violently with Monroe over the wisdom of switching on the fleet's engines. Monroe's military training pressed him to push further east, opening the distance between himself and any pursuing forces. By contrast, despite his darker moments

Smith seemed to be looking for time to hatch whatever he was scheming. The night before things had taken an unexpected turn when he had suddenly asked Monroe for *a complete, comprehensive, up-to-date breakdown* of the fleet in terms of the speed, firepower and carrying capacity –both in military and civilian terms- of each vessel in the armada. Despite much of the information being available in the ship's computer, Monroe and a small team had labored through the night up-dating and re-running the analysis to include those vessels which had joined them from the eastern seaports.
So it was that, after only a couple of hours sleep, he found himself waiting for Smith to appear on the bridge of *Genesis.* As usual, Smith had exercised his presidential prerogative of being late, though Monroe had disregarded the lack of courtesy and enjoyed the opportunity to watch the sun gliding ever higher into a cloudless sky. He stopped himself from asking, yet again, what the thinking had been behind his night's work. Such idle speculation would have simply spoilt the splendour of the new morning, and Monroe was so enraptured with the glories of the new day that it was only when he heard a slight coughing next to him that he realized that both Adams and Tuckman were standing by his side. The lieutenant was clearly deeply embarrassed,

a red hue filling his face and spreading down both sides of his neck. Tuckman had no such compunction. Without formality or greeting he simply said *The President has sent us for the analysis he asked you to do. He is too busy to come himself.*

Instantly, the faces of a dozen or more officers turned towards him, and Monroe found himself transforming into the same puce as Adams displayed. Brusquely, he proffered the heavy, sealed envelope he had been holding to Tuckman. T*he President knows where to find me if he wants to talk,* he added curtly, attempting to both hide the extent of the hostility he felt and to avoid meeting Tuckman's eyes. However, with the glass of the bridge to his rear, and the only escape from his humiliation blocked by the duo confronting him, Monroe had no choice but to barge his way through.

If Tuckman had thought that the admiral would prove a physically weak opponent, he immediately learnt his mistake. Monroe had worked out vigorously every day of his adult life, seen years of combat service and was galvanized by a seething anger. Whilst Tuckman was the professional body guard, in this situation his arrogance resulted in his being caught by surprise.

Monroe let his hand holding the enveloped drop, and then swept it up again on its edge as though to re-offer it. The weight of the envelope and the force behind it was more than enough to cut through whatever protection was afforded to Tuckman's crotch by the thin off-duty suit he was wearing. He gasped audibly, the pain causing tears to well briefly in his eyes, but by the time he could retaliate Monroe had already stuffed the envelope into Adams's hands and was striding from the bridge. It was Tuckman who found himself smarting as the crew smirked, despite their best efforts to hide their emotions.

Monroe immediately went to his cabin, sat down at his desk and poured a large whisky. It was the second of the morning, and looking in the mirror he reflected that his haggard face was showing the stresses of the near-constant tension with Smith. Taking another gulp from the glass, he tumbled from the chair into his bunk, kicked off his shoes and lay gazing at the white of the cabin ceiling.

The sun's light pouring through a porthole indicated that it was several hours later when Monroe awoke, and he immediately sensed a change in the speed and movement of the *Genesis.* Through they were now well clear of the Atlantic storm which had earlier bedeviled the armada, the power of the waves had been noticeable. Even on this, one of the largest ships the Christian Confederation commanded, ploughing through the waves had a distinct rhythm of its own. Now it was different, and Monroe immediately sensed that he was not feeling a change in the sea, but in *Genesis. 'What the hell is Smith doing now?'* he growled to himself. His was one of the few cabins with the luxury of running water, and swinging from the bunk he vigorously splashed some on his face in an attempt to counter the whiskey's effects.

He had reached the door and had his hand on the table when he stopped. Muffled voices penetrated the thick metal and it occurred to him that, if Smith had decided to take the opportunity to take complete control, he himself would be stopped by the security in the gangway. Then he could be diverted or held on some pretext until it was too late to argue. Not that arguing would necessarily do any good, but it would be the sort of direct confrontation that Smith abhorred, and Monroe still had considerable standing amongst the ranks and file.

Glancing around the cabin, it dawned on him that another luxury his seniority offered was a small – what could one call it? Not so much a balcony, but a small ledge? This had been left when this section of the ship had been refitted and his cabin built in an area which had once been a loading hatch.

Someone had thoughtfully welded a small guardrail to minimise the danger of falling the lethal distance to the ocean below. There had been odd occasions when Monroe had ordered the armoured door unsecured and he had been able to sit and enjoy breakfast or an evening meal whilst undisturbed and enjoying both the view and sea breeze.

The hatch's crude, reinforcing welds were covered by a large wall hanging of Christ on the Cross. This had been sewn by the WallWomen and given to Monroe as a personal present from Smith. Monroe was unsure whether Smith or any of his acolytes remembered the existence of the hatch and, if they did, whether they considered it to be of any importance. Most of *Genesis* utilised electronic locking keypads linked to the central security system, but by good fortune this hatch was secured with heavy securing bolts and locks.

The only key known to Monroe was kept in his desk drawer, though 'kept' was perhaps an inaccurate term to describe an object which had somehow survived the regular 'throw-outs' when Monroe tipped all and sundry into a bin when he found the clutter of the cabin intolerable. But this was where he had 'kept' it, and after a few seconds anxiously scrabbling through an assortment of files, the key was in his hands. He carefully unhung Christ, and within a minute the padlock was opened, the bolts heaved out of their locking positions. He cautiously slid it open the first few inches of its travel. Temporarily, the opening gave Monroe a –potentially- unjustified sense of relief that he was no longer a prisoner in his own accommodation.

He stopped and listened carefully. If the security detachment outside his door had been sufficiently attentive, they might have heard the rasping of poorly greased metal as both the bolt and hatch door were shifted. For now, it seemed their attention was elsewhere, for the door to the cabin stayed reassuringly closed.

He cautiously eased open the hatch further and peered out. Below, the ocean lazed gently, the swell bearing no witness to the severity of the storm they had left behind. A pair of seagulls wheeled over the waves. Rather than indicating the proximity of land, they were indicative of Smith's failure to totally eradicate the colonies which had nested in some of the more obscure corners of the armada's vast riggings and radar towers. Smith had deemed the presence of the birds as '*…demeaning the glory of God's armada…*' whilst Monroe had argued vehemently against the loss of life involved in sending sailors clambering amongst the ropes, cables and pulleys which often stretched remarkably haphazardly over a hundred feet into the air. This was a battle which Monroe had partly won, Smith having agreed that any nests in *'...especially inaccessible and dangerous places...'* should be left undisturbed, though the offending birds were to be shot whenever possible. A few ricochets from heavy armour, one fatal, had soon terminated this idiotic order.

Though Monroe could see only a tiny element of the fleet from his vantage point, it was immediately apparent that the vast majority of the vessels had been ordered to down their sails, and were riding gently on the waves. He could see only one vessel which was clearly under power, its sails downed to maneuver more readily through the fleet and cheap diesel smoke belching from its funnels. *'Simple idiocy if any Federal ships are near,'* Monroe muttered to himself. At this distance he could not make out the name of the ship, but the state of the engines suggested that it was one of the older vessels Smith and he had nominated as general fuel and cargo carriers. These were to be scuttled once their cargoes had been consumed by other vessels.

Consequently, he was about to dismiss this as a simple refuelling exercise when he was surprised to see a group of fast amphibious craft, each heavily laden with marines and weapons, bounce across the mile or so from *Genesis* and come alongside the belching carrier. No sooner had the marines clambered aboard using the webs slung over the side, than their transports was lifted aboard by the ship's cranes. They were followed by a second, third and fourth wave, and Monroe made a quick calculation that, allowing for twenty troops a boat, some five hundred must have made the transfer and the vessel had been loaded to full –or over-capacity.

Finally, a lone vessel with a skeleton crew made the journey. Despite the risk of being unbalanced and falling into the ocean, there was a single figure standing proudly at the bow holding the Presidential Pennant high. By now the ships had drifted closer, perhaps to less than half a mile, but even at this distance Monroe felt there was something disturbingly familiar about the profile.

Racing across the cabin, he was just able to return and focus his binoculars on the figure as the ship started to swing across the bow of *Genesis.* Through the lenses, he momentarily caught sight of Adams, the all-invasive presence since their departure from RougeWall. Even in the brief time Monroe had him in sight, he could clearly see the epaulets which had transformed the mere lieutenant into a full captain. Theoretically, only he could have approved such a promotion, so Smith had clearly decided to usurp his role. *What in hell is going on here?* he mumbled again to himself, both vocabulary and clarity of thought being limited by the alcohol.

Before he had time to answer his own question, he heard the sound of a key inserted in the cabin's door. Frantically, shoved the hatch closed but was too late to properly reaffix the Christ. He could only throw it crudely over its hanger before the door opened.

The man who entered was not the usual crew member who served Monroe, but glancing at his watch he realised to his surprise that his coffee was arriving exactly on time. *Good day Sir,* the steward greeted, saluting smartly whilst balancing a tray with a jug of steaming coffee and a pile of cakes on his other arm. *The President's compliments. He will be joining you shortly. He said that you should start without him,* and he inclined his head to the tray which contained two cups from the President's personal service.

Monroe was too surprised to respond, and after a brief pause the steward laid the tray on the admiral's desk, saluted again, and exited the cabin. He left Monroe with waves of conflicting emotions. At one level he feared that he was being invited to Smith's equivalent of the last supper, with himself being prepared for crucifixion, whilst at another the signals seemed to be that he was being forgiven for whatever transgression Smith believed he had committed. Finally, he poured himself a cup of coffee, sniffed at it suspiciously and, hesitating momentarily, took a large gulp. It tasted like RealCoffee, the first he had tasted in several days, and he decided –with no scientific basis- that if it were poisoned, a larger amount would end his agony more effectively than a small sip. Not that poisoning was part of Smith's traditional repertoire –his preference had always been for the public and dramatic-but recent events had convinced Monroe of the President's growing instability.

A slight tremor sent a ripple across the cup and some coffee lapped over the rim. '*Not a professional steward then, probably security,*' Monroe remarked to himself. His own steward had once explained, with considerable professional pride, how he had been trained to adjust the content of vessels according to the state of the sea- and never to fill to the rim. The tremor suggested that *Genesis was* once again underway, and the violence of the change suggested the use of engine rather than sail power. Despite the apparently imminent arrival of Smith, Monroe felt compelled to take one more look out of the hatch, and slid it open whilst effectively being hidden behind the *Christ.*

The ship's wake indicated that it was being steered hard to port, and as it turned a squadron of vessels sailing steadily to the east swung into sight, their sails full with the following wind. At the rear was the vessel Monroe had seen only a few minutes earlier, a slight whisper of diesel vapour hanging over it revealed that its engines had just been stopped. Ahead of it, a couple of destroyers were taking up a screening formation, though the evident lack of a rear guard immediately perplexed him.

Playing hide and seek with us Admiral? Or are you spying on the Lord's work? God forbid you would do such as UnChristian thing and just when the President has honoured you with his best coffee! The sneering voice was Tuckman's. Startled, Monroe almost fell out from behind the wall hanging to find that Tuckman and two Presidential Guards had entered the room whilst he had been busy observing the outside world. His immediate suspicion was that Tuckman had come to revenge himself for their earlier skirmish, but then the significance of *'Spying!'* sprung to mind. Given Smith's extreme paranoia, Monroe's life could be ended that very day if the word passed anyone's lips.

Less playing hide and seek than doing my duty to the Christian Confederation, Monroe spat back, deciding that attack was his only -desperate- choice. *I have sworn an oath before Holy God to guide and protect this fleet, and I have been imprisoned here and prevented from doing so for.....*

Well said John! Smith had entered the room unnoticed during the spat, looking visibly more relaxed than earlier in- was it the same day? He had clearly showered, his greying hair having temporarily lost much of its greasy lankiness, and a faint smell of patchouli pervaded the room. *Though I do take exception to the accusation of having imprisoned you,* Smith continued with a set smile. *It was simply felt that we,* and Smith inclined his hand inclusively towards Tuckman should introduce some additional security measures. *And for your safety we felt that you would be better in your cabin. Come now, do not let me waste my best coffee on you, though I do think that we should improve the security here, I was unaware how easy it was for someone to enter your cabin without security being alerted. Be so kind as to see to it immediately .... A slice of cake?* Monroe sensed he was safe- at least for the next few hours.

Chapter III
New Actors
12.49 UTC March 28th
43.6 degrees north, 58.7 degrees west

To say that Captain Henri Lagard of the Free Canada destroyer *La Cité du Québec* was displeased would have given a new nuance to the word in any available dictionary- not that a new one had been produced for nearly twenty years. His government had ordered him to assist his Federal American naval *'friends'* in '*...any way possible...*', and the way they had deemed possible had been to send him out into deep waters looking for something, though he hadn't been told exactly what. He had simply been ordered to communicate any contact, of any form, immediately to the Eastern Canadian navy's headquarters in Montreal. Unofficially, he had ordered his own intelligence officer to try and crack the American codes -not that he believed there was much chance of success, but at least he had gleaned enough data to give him a rough idea of where the main American forces were active.

As far as Lagard was concerned, the further he stayed from the Americans the better. He had been a young officer cadet on the *Halifax* when it had been sunk in the first Canadian-American hostilities over control over the Arctic oil fields. To his mind, the results had been partially beneficial with an upsurge in nationalism, the salvation of French-Canadian and increased defence spending. This had resulted, amongst many things, in the construction of the *La Cité du Québec.* The ship had been commissioned just as events were again becoming increasingly ugly and the, then Confederation, government had spared nothing in ensuring that – theoretically- she could match anything the US Federal Navy possessed in conventional warfare.

He looked again at the orders he had received, and a smile crept across his face. *La Cité's* assumed performance was much based on theoretical, technical specifications and the vessel had never been fully tested to her limits. Lagard himself had not been into true deep waters since the *Halifax* incident had limited most naval activity to close-shore coastguard-type activities. With its nuclear reactors purring and producing only twenty percent of their potential power, he had a sudden yearning to both push the ship and taste deep water. Canada's uranium reserves had been yet another sources of conflict with Washington, both official governments had struggled to control the remaining reserves during the religious wars.

One consequences of this access to the precious source of energy was that ten minutes later *La Cité* was heading east-southeast on a course which Lagard knew would sail well to the east of known Federal naval positions. The ship's design was essentially that of an enormous armed catamaran and in consequence it skipped across the western Atlantic at a speed which was all the more impressive for the lack of stress it was placing on the vessels engines. Unfortunately, a fortuitous failure in the communications system rendered the ship deaf to orders from anyone.

31.9 degrees north, 31.8 degrees west
12.49 UTC March 28th

Newly appointed Captain John Matthew Adams stood on the bridge of The Christian Confederation's heavily armed transport *Omega* with a smile on his face and a flutter in his heart. Since his childhood growing on the South Carolinian coast, his only desire had been to serve The Lord. Now, thanks to God and the wisdom of President Smith, God's anointed, his life's dream would be fulfilled at the age of only twenty five- he, John Matthew Adams, had been honoured with command of the President's '*special mission*'. Whilst the *Omega* enjoyed a lowly ranking in Smith's armada, being neither particularly fast nor heavily armed, Adams had been invited to set the presidential pennant on her in recognition of the special cargo she carried. Indeed, the crews and marines on all ships under his new command, and who had been selected for this mission, were all special. Adams mulled over the details of his mission again, content in the knowledge that most, if not all, of his command could be meeting their Lord God within the week.

Nuova Lisboa

22.01 UTC March 30th

Henry hadn't planned on sleeping with Marie-Claire. True, he had desired her from the moment they had met, attracted by the promise of her full breasts, her evident fitness and, to his mind, the inevitable- attraction of a blonde woman. Perhaps it was partly boredom after the failure of what the Europeans deemed a 'deep ocean scan' to find any trace of the Americans. Indeed, the deep ocean had been so empty that they had made contact with less than a handful of coastal vessels. Personally, Henry felt that they were not taking the situation entirely seriously. Though not a sailor himself, a bit of basics maths had led him to conclude that it was unlikely the Americans would have already neared the European coastline, even if they had experienced no delays. Now, he was lying with those same full breasts compressed against his chest and Marie-Clair's head snuggled against his shoulder. *'I wonder if she's sleeping with me to get information?'* he mused *' if so, I like the game.'* Not that he felt totally happy about the situation. He did have a wife and family back home and loyalty was one of the stated rules of the marriage – much stated on his wife's side but sadly neglected on his. He did try to be loyal, and loved his wife deeply, but days apart from Rachel always seemed to be months, and there was always this .....this need for a woman every other day.

Perhaps the desire for Marie-Claire had been partly generated by Amanda's behaviour. Initially, he had suspected that she slept around as a way of getting information, but had increasingly concluded that she was simply highly-sexed and extremely bored after having been stuck on this base for what she deemed to be *centuries.* She had directly propositioned Henry the night before, but despite her evident attractiveness, and the powerful effects of a bottle of red wine, he had declined the offer. It was one thing playing the field away from home, with little prospects of his wife discovering, but to have a government intelligence officer playing loose with that knowledge was an altogether more dangerous game; especially as it had transpired that she lived only a few blocks from their London home. Marie-Claire had been all the more attractive because of her obvious dislike for Amanda, and for a certain distance which made her even more attractive. That the chase had ended so swiftly left him wondering whether he was indeed '*irresistible*' - as both women had claimed- or whether all three were suffering from a certain ennui.

It seemed months rather than days since they had arrived in France, and then made their way down to Nuova Lisboa, and with each passing day he was less certain that he knew why he was here. He was deeply convinced - without any real evidence- that Smith would try to reach the old Christian lands. '*Perhaps Jerusalem? Or –where was it he was always ranting about at university?- Abyssinia perhaps. Smith was always saying that the true roots of Christianity could now be found there. Logically, the eastern Mediterranean was both more accessible and would give him the chance to prove himself against some of the Arab states. That*

would be Smith's style, giving his religious fanatics an opportunity to fight against other religious fanatics. God save the moderate and reasonable people who inadvertently got in the way! But what kind of reception would he receive there? Was there any evidence that he had links with the Zionist extremists who had run the government for the past ten years? He would have to ask Amanda about this.'

Whatever Smith was doing, it was not going to involve here and he was wasting his time – though increasingly pleasurable. Earlier that afternoon he had found himself musing that perhaps there were problems further south that the Europeans did not want them to see, and he had talked this over with Amanda. She who had mumbled something about the growth of *'...the great desert.'*, which was a term which he'd heard used a few years earlier to describe the spread of the Sahara into southern Europe. That had been as far as the conversation had progressed, and there was certainly no evidence of incontrollable drought conditions around Noava Lisboa. There were certainly plenty of irrigation dykes, Walls and dams, but he had seen no evidence that the crops could not support at least the local population. *What you thinking?* Marie-Claire murmured. *That was very good – you want again?* Henry hesitated briefly and then drove all thought of Smith from his mind as Marie-Claire rolled onto him. He had always liked being dominated in bed.

34.3 degrees north, 22.1 degrees west
13.22 UTC March 31st

La Malaga creaked ominously, but *La Malaga* always creaked. Its timbers had perhaps creaked when it had been built seventy or more years earlier, and perhaps the creaking had been one of the things

which had saved it from being requisitioned by somebody in power, or claiming to be in power, at some point during the past twenty or so years.
Now it wasn't so important that it creaked in the rolling waves, for it had brought in a reasonable living scouring the Portuguese and Spanish coasts for any surviving shoals. When this failed, forays followed further north in the Bay of Biscay, and as far south down the African coast as they dared with their fuel reserves. Relying on sail-power to outrun the western pirates was to invite death. Fernadez had met the pirates on several occasions as a gunner on a patrol boat in the Guarda Costas, the old coast guard, and had seen more than enough death and maiming in the ensuing gun fights. According to his father, the traditional problem on the Spanish coast had been people- running, initially for prostitution and illegal work, but as things had got worse environmental refugees had become a human wave which had filled the coffers of the pirates until they were sometimes better armed and equipped than state vessels.
So far, this fishing season had been unusually bad even by the standards of the repeatedly unusually bad, and so it was that Luis Ferdandez, Captain of *La Malaga*, had followed his ancestors in heading far out towards the once rich fishing grounds off the

Nova Scotian coast. Initially, the trip had been fruitless, but then good fortune and some costly high tech had led them into one of the largest shoals of tuna the crew had encountered for over a decade. Young, smallish fish it was true, but they bore witness to the potential resurgence of the fishing stocks after years in which their exploitation had been limited by the wars. But then fortune was a fickle beast, and they had scarcely filled the refrigerated holds and started their home trip when they were caught in a storm which had buffeted them for days. Then further disaster had struck. The engines failed, and there had been a desperate battle to start an old diesel compressor before the holds started to thaw.

Yet another change in their fortunes and a strong westerly had filled their sales, pushing them steadily homewards. The creaking was ominous however. Luiz could not remember a time when the holds had been so full, the ship so low in the water, and the creaking so .dangerous? He had considered reducing the sails to see if that made a difference, and had himself gone overboard to do an external inspection of the hull. He could find nothing wrong, though he had made a mental note there was enough encrustation to ensure a good week or two's work on the vessel in dry dock during the next winter. His eldest son would be able to help this time, Fernandez had decided, and perhaps would be able to join the ship for the following year. The entire family needed to work together to ensure a decent living, and it was time that the eldest stopped his reading and did some real work to put food on the table

Now, with a further strengthening of the westerly wind, he had decided to play safe and reduce his sails and thereby the pressure on the vessel. Inevitably, given the decrepitude of the vessel, one of the pulleys had blocked and he had ordered Juan Carlos, his most able crewman, to climb into the rigging to sort the problem. Juan Carlos had been named after one of the old Spanish kings, and was noted for his speed and ability in getting things sorted which other crew members struggled with. Now, he was being unusually sluggish.

'Que estas esperando Carlos?' What are you waiting for Carlos? Fernandez shouted, looking up at the figure perched some fifteen metres above his head. Rather than getting on the with the task in hand, Carlos was sitting, staring intently to the north east.

'Un veleio, capitano!', *A sail captain,* came the reply. *'No, dos veleios!'* *No, two sails!*

'Estan llegando por aqui?' Coming this way? Luiz demanded, immediately aware of their vulnerability.

La Malaga carried a couple of heavy machines guns for protection, but against two ships...?

No sure capitano, Carlos replied, dropping back into the semi-English dominant even in much of the south. *Looks like there perhaps three, or four sails- or perhaps a very big ship. They started commercial sailings again?! I climbing up rigging to see. Wait!* The minute or so that it took Carlos to negotiate the next five metres to the very top of the mast seemed an eternity. Luiz had not seen another vessel this far out for at least two years..... and as for two or three? Well, that would be going back ten years or more before the Great Storms had started. So who was out here with them now?

Capitano, you no believe this!! Carlos shouted *I see sails of five, perhaps six ships. Not fishing vessels I know. Maybe we take sails down?* The logic was impeccable. Only military vessels could afford radar, so if they could get their sails down fast enough they might escape notice. The alternative was to dump their hard-earned catch and to try to out-run whoever it was. Luiz was not going to lose this full hold.

Ok lads! he shouted to his crew *Everything down quick now. Best time, like we do in drills!* Within five minutes, deprived of its sails, *La Malaga* was wallowing in the sea. Despite his immediate concerns, in the relative silence Luiz noted with concern the distinct creaking suggesting that even the sail-less mast was transmitting pressure to the keel. La Malaga's days were numbered without massive expenditure, which he could ill afford.

Luiz, one of the crewmen said, tapping him on his shoulder, *have a look*. Whilst Fernandez ran a friendly ship, at sea he was clear about rank and discipline and was shocked at the unexpected informality - even though it came from one of the English renegades. One look at the seaman's face told him that there was something seriously amiss. Taking the old binoculars from him, he focused on the north easterly horizon.

Oh God! He exclaimed. *There must be thirty or more of them. They are in battle formation if I see right. And the flag? Anyone know the flag?* Minutes later he was in his cabin with *La Malaga*'s first mate. The choices were relatively simple. With luck, their presence would not be noted, and they would be able to sail home undisturbed. However, who knew what damage could be wreaked on the European coast if the ships they had spotted continued with their course? It had been instantly, unanimously agreed that this was a military formation, not a fishing expedition, and they were flying a new American flag. Luiz was surprised how quickly all had agreed that they should radio their information home, even though it seemed that their home port was not the destination of this group. Now the problem was how to do it.

La Malaga had a set for inshore communications, but he hadn't used the long range system for so long that he was unsure either that it was serviceable or that he remembered how to use it. And what exactly was he going to say and to whom. Looking though his manual, he found the old frequency for emergency communications, recognising it vaguely from his days with the coast guard, but had a major doubt if it still functioned given all the cut backs. The set was another problem. He suddenly remembered having scavenged the mains plug for something else, and it took a bit of prodding and a lot of sparks before he could get a steady hum and a row of lights which suggested that it was working. *Cartagena central, this is the ship La Malaga at 34.3 degrees north, 22.1 degrees west. We have in sight over thirty suspected American ships on a bearing of... he started*, and never finished, as a missile from the Christian Confederation cruiser *Houston* shredded *La Malaga* and its crew into millions of tiny pieces.

34.2 degrees north, 22.0 degrees west
14.49 UTC March 31st

Monroe had never seen Smith so wild, not even at his wildest. Literally frothing at the mouth, he was almost running back and forwards across the bridge of the *Genesis*, shouting questions and orders to which he brooked no reply and waited for none. Less than an hour earlier the two men had been sitting, drinking coffee and eating cakes like a couple of reconciled old friends who had met for the first time in years at a church tea party on a Sunday afternoon. Smith's mood had changed instantly when he had taken a call, and rather than explain events to Monroe had stormed out of the cabin, simply shouting *Follow me!*

The result had been a brief, armed stand-off. Some of the marine guard were still under the impression that Monroe was confined to his cabin, whilst Tuckman's men attempted to follow Smith's orders and lead Monroe to the bridge. Monroe silently prayed that one of the numerically superior marine guards would be sufficiently nervous to open fire on Tuckman and his squad. But God was not on his side at this juncture, and a brief call to Smith's security had defused the situation and allowed Monroe to join Smith on the bridge. Pandemonium reigned. Heads turned as he arrived, and Monroe was pleased to observe that all of the naval crew saluted and stood to attention until told to stand easy. Here there was still loyalty, though uncertainty as to who commanded. Faces turned from Monroe to Smith and, he noted with surprise, to Tuckman.

Who failed to spot the vessel? Smith demanded instantly. A stream of questions followed, focusing on who had been in command at the time, and whether the unidentified vessel had been able to broadcast before being eliminated. Monroe noticed that Tuckman became increasingly tense as Smith repeatedly asked the same questions. It occurred to him that Tuckman may actually have been given command of the fleet, but had chosen to visit Monroe instead of staying on the bridge. If that were indeed the case, it would be interesting to see how Smith reacted. Monroe almost smiled as he realised that even Smith's logic would find it hard to blame himself for this situation, given that he had been confined to his cabin on Smith's orders.

Finally, Smith had shouted something about *Go and see if there are any survivors, I want no loose ends!* and had stormed out. Tuckman followed, giving a backward glance as he left the bridge which, for the first time ever, seemed to communicate an element of fear in the man. Then something changed. 'The evil bastard's going to find someone to blame and Smith will help him,' Monroe thought to himself and he had started to make a list of likely victims – doubtless chosen for their lack of warm praise for

Smith rather than any responsibility – when he became aware of the total silence on the bridge.

And? he had addressed the most senior officer.

Christian Admiral Sir, are you in command? The officer replied tentatively. *Or are we waiting instructions from Mr. Tuckman or the President? Can I assume that we are to look for survivors? I understand that was our Christian President's last order?*

Then we shall follow it. It seems wise to understand more fully what has happened and I believe the wind will carry us there, will it not? Please set course. Several minutes later Monroe was standing surveying the ocean, nursing the cup of coffee his own purser had rescued from the relics of his meeting with Smith, when the same officer walked slowly over to him. Monroe knew him as a former regular navy lieutenant who had converted, joined the Confederation's navy and been rapidly promoted by Monroe himself on the basis of merit rather than favouritism.

Permission to speak Christian Admiral. Monroe looked directly at the man. He was what? About twenty eight, so had seen almost eighteen years of on-and-off conflict.

Permission granted Jason, he replied, using the man's Christian name to reassure.

Permission to speak frankly admiral? Jason replied, lowering his voice.

Permission granted. What troubles you?

Admiral, Sir, what is going on? When we set sail from RougeWall there seemed to be a mission and a common purpose. I think that if you spoke to most of the crew now they would say that our own leadership is divided by the pursuit of individual power and ...

Careful son, Monroe said firmly. This could be a trap or a genuine concern. *Don't talk yourself into danger. You know* he said, emphasising the words and looking the other man straight in the eyes, *that President Smith claims – has* he corrected himself *-direct guidance from Our Lord. There may be differences of detail, but we all share the common good. As to exactly what we are doing at present...mmm. I do believe the Lord can lead us in mysterious ways, and our ultimate destination is still a mystery-even to myself. And, as admiral there, are those who might think I should know what is going on in heaven,* he added laughingly. *So please excuse me now, I have duties to attend to.* Later, Monroe had asked himself if the officer had noted his careful use of words. He had directly inserted *claims* to replace has and *the common good* to replace *the common goal.* Neither change might be deemed significant in daily conversation, but an intelligent, attuned person would have noted the change. Equally, because they were not precise repetition of Smith's words, for some they would have formed the basis for interrogation for heresy.

37.4 degrees north, 23.5 degrees west
20.09 UTC March 31st

To say that Lagard was any less displeased than Smith would have been far from the truth – but this was contained beneath a professional veneer. His government had ordered him to assist his Federal American, naval *'friends'* in '...any way possible...', and that had provided him with a wonderful opportunity to test the *La Cité* in a way which had been denied him in the past. True, as he sadly noted in his log, there had been a major, convenient, communications failure which had prevented him from either contacting the *'fucking yankees'* or his own government, but he felt a personal certainty that this would soon be remedied when they turned towards home.

He had decided to do this at first light of the following day. The wind and currents had been favourable on their journey east, but the headwinds would make the journey back slower despite the power of the ship's engines - and he had promised the crew they would have shore leave the next weekend. So, tomorrow morning would be the last time in terms of performing his orders to help the Americans, and the contradictory order from naval command –carefully sealed in his drawer- ordered him to release his crew for leave by 16.00 on Friday.

If Lagard had been both more experienced in deep ocean sailing, and more careful, he would have discovered that he was not actually where he believed himself to be. It was not enough of a difference to be of great significance in terms of arriving home on time, though in coastal waters it might have been the difference between a port and a rock. Out here, he had been a bit crude in his estimates, knowing that the minutiae made no difference in what was essentially an opportunity to play what his father had called ...what was it again *'boy racers'?* Though he lacked specific information about the Americans he was hunting, he felt confident he could cause them considerable damage if he caught them under sail. Speed was his great ally. He had found the last few days surprisingly tiring. In part, it was the novelty of open-sea navigation without satellite. He had been taught solar navigation of course, but his very early career had relied totally on satellite navigation until the first Electronic Wars had removed that luxury. He could still remember when, as a sign of things to come, a huge Japanese oil tanker had sailed onto the remnants of The Great Australian Barrier Reef rather than into harbour in Japan. In theory, navigation was not one of his principle responsibilities, but it had soon become evident that his other senior officers doubted their own capabilities in this field. Hence, navigating had proved quite demanding in its own right and then there was the energy drain arising from the potential for actual action against the enemy. Perhaps it was this tiredness which had caused one of his early errors which, like many early mariners, had caused him to drift slightly but incrementally further and further from his intended course.

Lagard was about to end his shift and go to the mess for a bite before retiring to his cabin, when an entry from the ship's log earlier in the day caught his attention. He had left the bridge to deal with a disciplinary issue, and to his irritation found that he had not been informed of a brief communication burst detected by his ship's intelligence section. Whilst he was not above disobeying orders himself, the one things he would not tolerate under his command was sloppiness. *Mullard!* he shouted to his first officer at the other end of the bridge. *Why didn't you tell me about this transmit around 13.30? And what's the context?*

Didn't think it was worth mentioning sir. Probably some garbled stuff from the other side, so we..

Didn't think was the right part lieutenant, Lagard spat back, struggling to retain his calm. *Anything this far out may be of value. I want all the info we have on this frequency and a decrypt of the message before anyone goes to their bunks. Understood? Even if we have to stay up all night. And I want it done well or all shore leave is cancelled ...off. Fini! Clear?* was his parting shot as he headed towards the mess for his evening meal.

Chapter IV
Dawn
37.1 degrees north, 23.0 degrees west
05.12 UTC April 1st

Lagard sat with his strategic and tactical teams in *La Cité's* tactical situation room. It was unusually cramped, with sufficient space for every officer only after some of the lower ranks had been ordered to the bridge. He was still tired, though he had slept for several hours. Overnight, he had ordered the ship powered down whilst he decided what to do next, so their forward progress had been relatively little- probably a mistake because the reduced momentum and noise had changed the habitual background to his sleep, and made it all the more intermittent. By contrast, some fatigued faces in the room reflected the stresses of a full night spent trying to reassemble a brief, garbled message which had been plucked from the ether by *La Cité*s highly sensitive antennae. He looked at the finished work again.

You sure about this? he enquired of Mullard, who simply nodded his head in the direction of Singh, the ship's head of electronic warfare.

Lieutenant Singh did the work sir, and he is nearly a hundred percentage sure that is what it says. Isn't that right Singhie? We checked with both the computers and a couple of Spanish speaking crew. They reckon it's mainland Spanish, not Amero-Spanish. We got one crew with parents from Mexican ancestry and another from Chile, and they're both sure it's not an American area accent.

And you are confident that they were talking about American ships? And about the coordinates? Lagard demanded. *We have no evidence of a reply? Any suggestions as to why the messages stopped like that?*

Could be anything captain, Singh replied. His slight Scottish resonance continued to mark out the eastern provinces from the mainland. *Could be we just got a lucky bit because of atmospherics, could be their equipment, or perhaps…well, perhaps the Chrissies didn't like them talking to the world and blocked their system. Easily done.*

Suggestions? Lagard shot, hopeful that his officers would, for once be in agreement. As captain, he did, indeed, have the final word, but a democratic propensity had developed in the Canadian forces during the wars, and Lagard strongly favoured keeping at least his officers on board.

With respect captain, Mullard replied immediately, *I don't know what your orders were exactly, but I gather they were to try and locate some Christian American ships-and to destroy them? I don't think you'd find a member of this crew who would object to that, but …but, if we could solve our communications problem…* and he was forced to stop as the entire table burst into laughter. *As I was saying before I was rudely interrupted,* he continued, his freckled face red through trying to control his own laughter *it might be wise to let navy headquarters know what little we know. Perhaps it's something which would help create a larger picture for the Intel. Until we get orders, perhaps we could go look at the coordinates this boat gave? Could be useful.*

An excellent suggestion Alan. I might even remember to forget your fuck up yesterday if you continue like this! Lagard smiled. His was a good crew, and their mistakes came from lack of experience, not good will. *Any other suggestions? No? OK. Meeting finished.* Within half an hour communications had been fortuitously re-established, a message sent to naval headquarters in Montreal, and the ship was sailing at full speed towards the coordinates broadcast by *La Malaga.*

29. 2 degrees north, 18. 5 degrees west

04.49 UTC April 2nd

Newly-appointed Captain John Matthew Adams stood on the bridge of The Christian Confederation armed transport *Omega* trying to hide his growing concern. To the north, clouds were forming ominously, a portent of yet another storm and a potential hindrance to their work. Of immediate concern was the fact that the coast was now visible, his men ready to go ashore, and still he had not received his final orders from his President Smith. Every second's delay increased the risk of their being spotted by the enemy and while fully confident that, with God's support, he would be able to overwhelm any local resistance, he was also highly aware of the crucial role of timing and precision in the mission. Delay also increased the risk of reinforcements arriving, but without the President's orders he dared not initiate the mission. His daily prayers since leaving the main fleet had been both for the safety of the main body, but also to minimise the losses amongst his own men. Smith had assured him that every man who fell for the cause would immediately go to heaven, but having personally experienced the misery inflicted by the loss of loved ones, Adams had a strong, personal desire to spare suffering amongst the families which his command had left behind.

Orders? Christian Captain Sir, enquired the deck communications officer. *The other ships are asking if they should start loading the landing craft.* Adams hesitated. He knew the heavy equipment would take time to unload into the landing crafts once the marines had set out, so time was of the essence. His own intelligence were attempting to block all communications out of the island, and it was unlikely that the mainlanders would be willing or able to send much support, but – as he had decided only seconds earlier- delay increased the risks. *Give the order. Omega is to commence.*

Spaniards had settled on Las Palmas during the 15th century. It had seen starvation when the crops failed, witnessed the coming and going of ships as the sea routes to the New World grew, and had become a popular tourist resort during the late 20th and early 21st centuries. Tourism came to be the backbone of the local economy, though it had declined dramatically with the start of The Troubles. Initially, the wealthy had continued to come to the island from mainland Europe for some winter sun, but the start of the Great Storms and pirate raids from the African coast had crippled the it both economically and socially. With a high dependence on food imports, the disruption and first tastes of true hunger had resulted in the majority of the population migrating to the mainland, many finding work as labourers in the construction of the early Walls. Behind, they left cities and other settlements which were now either partly submerged by the rising ocean or starting to witness successful re-colonisation by the island's vegetation.

Despite all the retrenchments, the Confederation and Madrid had decided that the geographical location of the Canaries was valuable in providing weather forecasts for the fishing fleets. This role had initially increased in importance as access to reliable satellite data had declined during the Electronic Wars, though the fishing fleets now remained ever closer to the shore. Regardless, the island still hosted a team of some twenty climatologists who rotated on a six-monthly basis, and a detachment of a hundred and sixty marines charged with protecting the climatologists, government officials and local population against raiders coming up the African coast. Fortunately, much of the island rose steeply out of the sea, so that there had been no additional Wall costs despite the rising sea level.

Until the previous year it had been seen as a good posting, with a substantial, unofficial trade in electronics from the Chinese-West African Cooperation Zone. One of the great early luxuries had been unrestricted electricity, thanks to a highly efficient solar power system installed just before The Troubles, but much of this had been wrecked in a Super Storm the previous year. The result had been a dramatic decline in both the Chinese trade and the merits of a posting. The changes had been a major source of disappointment amongst the troops and climatologists who were nearing the end of their tour. Historically, they would have been able to return home with a range of difficult-to-find items which would have brought good prices and considerable status at home. This time, only one Chinese trader had bothered - or dared- to make the run during their six month tour, so there was little to take home to boost an increasingly modest pay. Whilst the weather centre was located at the old tourist airport, the marines were garrisoned on the eastern side of the island, an area less exposed to the savagery of the wind when a Storm developed. So it was that when the men and women of the 1st Christian Marine Corp stormed ashore on the west coast of the island, the only inhabitant to be aware of their arrival was a stray dog which had taken to sleeping amongst a pile of rotting deck chairs driven far up the beach by the storms. Within thirty minutes the marines had established a secure beach head and the first landing craft were heading shore ward, full of armoured transport and other cargo, and with them came Captain Adams. He walked solemnly down the ramp of the landing craft holding the Presidential Pennant aloft and, with a smile on his face, shouted jubilantly *God is with us. Praise be to God.*

33.1 degrees north, 20.2 degrees west

05.59 UTC April 2nd

Lagard had woken early, feeling an enormous sense of frustration. They had spent the previous morning scouring the ocean for any evidence of the apparent sinking of this Spanish ship, and by mid-afternoon had been forced to a totally irrelevant conclusion- the sea was much cleaner than it had been before The Troubles. The latter had effectively curtailed long-distance travel for all but diplomatic missions and the odd business mogul's convoy risking a Calm Season expedition. Then, Mullard had taken the navigation readings for the first time that trip, had looked at Lagard's chart, and had saved the captain the public humiliation of being reminded that he needed to work from the ship's chronometer in making calculations and not from his wrist watch. The difference between the two was now fifteen minutes, enough to add a substantial error when navigating over the vast distances of the Atlantic. Working from the new estimated, it had taken them less than an hour to locate an oil slick and splinters of wood sufficient to suggest that a significant vessel had gone down in the vicinity.

Lagard's second frustration arose from the lack of reply from Montreal. This was ironic given his initial decision to have a communications 'problem' of his own, but now he could only speculate that some important discussions were taking place between the government and the military, and perhaps there were even discussions about how to use the

American's apparent, new desire for cooperation as a leverage to get them out of occupied Canadian territory.

So it was that, uncertain as to what to do, and with the vague thought that they might still try to make a weekend's furlough, he had eased the engines back once again. He had thought of the possibility of re-contacting naval headquarters, but both chronology –the politicians would be fast asleep – and the security risk inherent in repeated transmissions, had decided him against this. He was turning restlessly once again in his bunk when there was a hesitant knock at the door. *Come in*! Lagard shouted, sitting up just as a young ensign entered the room. *Sorry to disturb you captain. Compliments of the watch officer. There is a priority message from Montreal.*

Las Palmas

06.37 UTC April 2nd

The troops stationed on Las Palmas were commanded by a career officer who had seen service with Eurocorp service in the wars of The Troubles, had been twice wounded in skirmishes with both Jewish and Arab units during the struggles over Mediterranean trade routes, and then –in a development which shocked her entire understanding of reality – had fought with the European troops allied with the Turks, Israeli and

United States Federal forces in the first conflicts in which extreme elements in the US forces had forged an alliance with Zionist fanatics.
This, set against the shortages and seasonal unpredictability of recent decades had totally upturned her world view, which had once been firmly rooted in Spanish Catholicism. Both her father and grandfather had served in the military; her grandfather had been in what was then Brussels as an officer with the old NATO organisation and her father one of the first Spanish officers to serve with the developing Eurocorp. Now, after over thirty years' service, long over-due retirement and with a lingering feeling that she should have become a mother at some stage in her life, Anna-Maria Jiminez was a tired, if not bitter, woman.
Her early morning mood was not greatly helped when there was a loud rap at her door and a marine sergeant strode in without the slightest pause. *Sorry to disturb you* he gasped *but there is fighting.*
Fighting? she demanded, with little concern but making a mental note that her men needed more physical training. *Between whom? This is a pirate attack?*
No captain. We have a call that civil police are attacked by American soldiers.

Nuova Lisboa
06.57 UTC April 2nd

In his youth, out on the eastern coast, Henry had caught his father viewing some porn on an old recording system –a VCD, or something like that was it? At the time he'd been both shocked to think that his father could want anyone other than his mother, but then -like most children – had found himself even more shocked to think of his parents engaging in anything like the scenes on the screen. In a way he had also been rather amused by the pathetic plot of the pornography which had involved lots of women and one man in uniform at the start, and lots of women and one man – all without uniform and engaged in various unbelievable acts of Olympian sex – by the end.

This morning he was, for the first time, starting to feel something of the excitement which a woman in uniform could engender for him. For the first time he'd stayed over-night in Marie-Claire's accommodation, and had found the act of watching her dress so stimulating that he had spent the last five minutes pressing her to miss role call and declare herself sick. She has resisted, at first vigorously and then with the first signs of weakening as he entreated her with offers of what he knew he could not deliver – but Olympian sex seemed like a good idea at this time of the morning when Henry was at his best. His latent victory was snatched away by a loud knock at the door and, without a second's delay Amanda barged in followed by two burly military policemen. *Henry darling, so glad to find you*, she purred *we have been looking for your everywhere for the best part of ten minutes! Very naughty of you to have left your accommodation without telling someone, but I do understand,* and she shot a glance at Marie-Claire. *Nice to see you too hun up, and dressed, though I'm shocked to see you leaving Henry to play military at this early ...*

Get to the fucking point Amanda! Henry snapped, his frustration over-ridding any elements of courtesy he felt towards the woman. *What do you and your friends want?'* he added, indicating the two MPs who, though they may not have understood every word, were enjoying the domestic drama.

Ah, a good point Henry. I come – what is the old expression? Yes, I come bearing news of our American friends, she proclaimed proudly, and with emphasis to demonstrate her pride in knowing what she considered a famous quote.

Henry looked blankly and then shot *The Christian or non-Christian variety? Fried or roasted?* Henry shot, half rising from the bed before he realised he was still totally naked. The younger of the two MPs had clearly lost the plot linguistically, but he struggled to repress a smile as Marie-Claire visibly blushed.

Smith, half-baked variety, Amanda replied instantly. Whatever she had been doing that night it had not involved sufficient alcohol to slow her this morning. *But do tell, what would be your best guess for an American landing?*

A landing? and he lurched naked from the bed and started dragging on his clothes amidst Amanda's giggles. *So soon? It must be on the southern Spanish or Moroccan coast so that they can control access. I'm right?*

Nope, and because I like you I'll not make you guess and shall put you out of your misery. They've landed in the Canary Islands. Now, I don't know my religion so well, but what the hell have those islands got to do with Smith and his bloody beliefs? Anyway, the big guy wants to see you now, so you'll get working on ideas, won't you?

34.2 degrees north, 21.0 degrees west
06.59 UTC April 2nd

Once again Monroe stood on the bridge of *Genesis.* Once again he balanced a cup of coffee in his hands, though this time it was the usual LikeCoffee rather than the real stuff Smith had honoured him with. Once again he felt sick, but this time was different. Despite the religious convictions which had first attracted him to the Christian Cause, and despite the adoration he had initially felt for the President,

Monroe felt he was sliding into a living hell from which he could see no escape.

He had hoped and prayed that Smith would not look for innocent scapegoats for the incident with the ship they had sunk. Within his own command there had initially been unanimous agreement that Tuckman had been left in command for those vital minutes and that he had abandoned the bridge for reasons unknown – to extract vengeance on himself Monroe suspected, and he wondered idly what would have happened if Smith had not come to his cabin at that precise time.

Then it had been discovered that the vessel had started to transmit details of their location and the order had been issued to hold a full inquisition. Inevitably, voices had immediately fallen silent. Equally, inevitably Tuckman had found the scapegoats to be sacrificed for his error; doubtless these were men and women who had –knowingly or otherwise- offended Smith or Tuckman or one of their close ones at some point in the past. Inevitably, those accused had been found guilty and Smith had made a point of ensuring that they were hung from the yardarms of the 'guilty' ship in the macabre replication of 18th century naval punishment which Monroe was increasingly convinced provided Smith with some form of pleasure.

The entire thing was ridiculous. The *Raleigh* was simply a Soul carrier -150 passengers plus crew- which had joined the fleet after RougeWall. It had been stationed towards the rear of the armada, had not been involved in fleet defence and was vastly inferior in technological terms to many of the vessels in the fleet. The captain and crew lacked the protection which long-contact with the fleet awarded others, and –as Tuckman himself had observed- the inquisition's methods were such as to encourage the bravest man to change his version of reality within a matter of minutes. Certainly the captain and his senior officers had withstood less than twenty minutes of Tuckman's 'pressure techniques' before they signed a confession with some ridiculous story, totally removed from actual events, about how they had intended to separate themselves from the fleet and inform the enemy vessel of the armada's destination and intent.

The entire thing was so ridiculous –it was known that even Monroe was not privy to Smith's Revelation, or was it Revelations?- and that the Admiral had come under intense pressure from many senior fleet officers to intervene. Not that anyone risked contradicting the story, but the plea was for Christian clemency. Consequently the day had been characterised by signals flashing up and down the line and two captains even daring –with a subsequent, immediate demotion to the ranks- to break radio silence as the day wore on. Monroe's professionalism would not tolerate indiscipline, and though he felt increasingly estranged from Smith his loyalty to The Lord's Souls was undiminished. Amongst the lower ranks and Souls the rumour was deliberately spread by Tuckman's agents that there had been a plot, that President Smith had thwarted it with God's guidance, and that they were continuing their mission.

The information trickling back to Monroe was that there was some incredulity this time and that morale was falling. The vast majority of Souls aboard had no experience of the sea, and were feeling disillusioned after weeks at sea, much of the time entombed below deck with the stench of sea-sickness vomit. *Justice for agreeing to this mystery tour,* had been Monroe's initial, bitter reaction/ Later, he had to moderate his sentiments as his own honesty forced him to admit that he had been one of the first, and most loyal, exponents of this same *'mystery tour'*.

Smith had refused to see him, and by evening the three 'ring leaders' of the conspiracy had been hung from the yardarms of the *Raleigh*. No naval court had been involved, so the entire process lay outside of Monroe's competence. He had been with Smith in the President's cabin while the executions were taking place, his mind fully focused on the contents of the meeting. Smith had finally explained his plans. He didn't share the minutiae with Monroe; Smith loved having his little secrets, not least because of the power they gave him. What Monroe got was the broad sweep- enough to understand why Adams had sailed away with his own flotilla and enough to understand that Smith's intent was no less than to obliterate the Wuccie Federal United States. Only the eastern states would be involved, but Smith explained carefully that the material and psychological damage would be such as to bring any surviving Wuccie enclaves to their knees, permitting a swift Christian victory in the east. Subsequently, the Christian forces would be able to turn their attention to the decadents in California and the north west. What Monroe got was a vision of events which Smith compared, alternating between Sodom and Gomorrah and a place called Carthage.

Monroe had to check *'Carthage'* on the ship's data after the meeting. He was in no mood to admit any ignorance before Smith and, especially, Tuckman. Sodom and Gomorrah was understandable instantly, for Smith would be The Lord's tool in annihilating the Wuccies. 'Carthage' was an interesting read, and Monroe was quick to note the similarities between the Roman's deliberately seeding of land with salt to render it sterile, and the medium and long-term consequences of Smith's plans.

Initially, Monroe had been filled with admiration at the absolute simplicity of what Smith had told him, and could only wonder that none of the historical terrorist groups had attempted this. But around two in the morning he had woken from a nightmare, drenched in a cold sweat. The vision had been that of mile after mile of bleak fields, littered with skulls and bones. Somehow, these had grown flesh and blood, revealing the faces and forms of their original owners. Monroe had found himself walking through this terrifying landscape, and as he did so the women and children had turned on him, screaming and clawing at him and united in their condemnation of him as a mass murderer.

Awake, Monroe had poured himself a double whiskey and sat shaking on his bunk. His instincts and training were those of the professional military over-lying, sometimes combined with, and sometimes in conflict with, the Christian sentiments of mercy and justice he had imbibed from his parents. It was true - Smith's plan was a brilliant way of ending the conflict with few further losses of

Christian Souls. But, it was nothing less than mass extermination with no differentiation made between young and old, combatant and non-combatant, Wuccie and Believer. And what of the many thousands of Believers –both free and imprisoned - still living in the Federal lands? All were doomed if Smith succeeded, and the contradictions of his military training and religious beliefs left him greatly troubled. It would indeed be a great victory, but one which would leave a stench in the nose of human history. And would The Lord approve?

He spent the rest of the night mulling over the implications and morality of Smith's plans, and was so pre-occupied with them that he had failed to notice a change in the speed of the *Genesis* until he went on bridge that morning. The duty officer explained that President Smith had personally come to the bridge in the early hours, and ordered that the entire fleet be slowed so that the Raleigh could take the lead position. As they were talking the Raleigh slowly eased past them far off on the starboard side, its sails bulging. Then, as the ship's bells sounded for 07.00 reveille, the time when the crews would be mustering for roll call and many of the Souls would be coming on deck for fresh air, the *Raleigh's* sails were drawn up by their huge mechanical winches, revealed three bodies dangling from the nooses attached to the highest masts.

What do you think John Christian? Do you feel that this is a suitable reminder of the need for discipline at all times? Despite the vanguard of Presidential Guards, Smith had arrived on the deck without Monroe noticing. Automatically, Monroe stood to attention and saluted, spilling much of the LikeCoffee down his leg and soiling his naval whites in the hasty transfer from right to left hand. *Careful now Admiral,* Smith laughed shallowly *can't afford any more slip ups can we?*

Certainly not Mr. President, Sir, Monroe replied, noting the inherent threat. I do have one question though. After our discussion last night I understood there was a need to make some considerable speed, but I also understand you ordered the fleet to slow so that this... and he hesitated before inclining his head to the *Raleigh. Just for clarity, and to avoid any 'slips' as you rightly say, I assume this change has been communicated to what you referred to last night as The other party?'*

Momentarily, there was a look of incomprehension on Smith's face and then panic. *Of course admiral,* he replied hurriedly, stress clearly evident in his voice. *Would I forget such an important thing? Now, if you could excuse me, I have much to do. And may I remind you to ensure that every ship in the fleet is instructed to observe the fate of those traitors on the Raleigh. I shall see you in due course later today.*

With that Smith hurried off, pushing through the exit from the bridge before his guards could take position. '*Would you forget such an important thing, my ass,*' Monroe observed to himself. '*He was so busy covering Tuckman, and perhaps getting a thrill from the executions, that he's forgotten to contact Adams. He will find someone else to blame though.*'

Finishing the last dregs of the LikeCoffee, Monroe gave orders for all fleet crews and Soul complements to assemble on deck as the Raleigh held her position and the remaining elements of the fleet sailed past her. At one level he despised himself for his inability to prevent events such as this, and the squandering of lives which had shown their love and loyalty to the Cause. Simultaneously, he was convinced that his own fall from power would unleash a much darker side of Smith's personality, though he now questioned if this was possible after the revelations of the previous evening. The danger signals were there in relation to his own position. Smith had never mentioned his intention to have the entire fleet review the corpses and '*...his may I remind* you...' was part of what Monroe had come to recognise as part of Smith's daily armoury for creating uncertainty and blaming others for his own errors.

He hesitated for a second before crossing to the vessel's main computer console. Amongst many functions this contained detailed data on the maximum speed of every ship in the armada. Systematically collected, it included variants for wind, wave heights and draught, and, based on this data, instructions could be given to each ship on the amount of sail to unfurl to achieve a specific speed. This was the data which Monroe now ordered communicated to every vessel. He could not stop this grotesque charade, but he could shorten it by increasing the speed of the fleet. Moreover, if what Smith had told him last night was true, Smith would have no choice but to be thankful for this initiative. Time was now of the essence if Adams and his team were to succeed, though no sooner had Monroe found himself thinking this than another part of his mind was praying for his failure.

Looking at the main navigation charts, Monroe ordered a minor change in course and noted the change in the Genesis as her sails swelled with the increase in wind. Looking to the north, he noted that the sky seemed to be ever more threatening, and another thought entered his mind. Successful or not, Adams would provoke the European into looking for the source of the attack on their territory. If Adams failed in his primary objective, and the Europeans failed to realise the intent of the attack, they might just shrug it off as an irritating – but very bizarre - sally into their back yard. However, if they had any idea of what was planned, then they would muster every ship and aircraft they could to hunt down and destroy Monroe's command. And God alone knew what was behind them. Had their attack on WashingtonWall been largely disregarded, or had Lopez ordered what was still the considerable might of the United States Federal Government's Atlantic fleet to seek and destroy them?

Looking again at the consoles, Monroe was forced to consider that his huge fleet contained tens of thousands of innocent Souls, and that these were his responsibility. True, he had some excellent fighting vessels, but many of his command were converted civilian ships with little or no armour and inexperienced crews to man the weapons systems. Turning back offered the near certainty of encountering the Federal navy and, if Adams was successful, near certain death. Hesitation offered the near certainty of encountering the European navy. Whilst this had been severely mauled in past conflicts, the limited data available indicated that the

European had been rapidly improving their fighting capacity. Again though, Monroe recognised that this was an empty discussion- Adams's success would ensure death where they now sailed. No, the only hope now was to sail forward at the highest possible speed and pray that the Lord -and his weather- would be with them.

Nuova Lisboa

07.39 UTC April 2nd

Henry had found himself making a comparison between the base and an angry beehive as he had been marched the three hundred metres or so from Marie-Claire's accommodation to the main admin block. Marched? Yes, he had found himself marching rather than walking. The MPs' patience seemed to have been exhausted once the amusement of early morning domestics and reverse strip- tease had worn off.

It had started to rain heavily when they were half way, and Henry noted the way in which the technicians hesitated in loading the fighters and bombers into their cradles, casting a wary eye to the sky. He had already learnt enough from his time with the European military to know that long-distance flights were as dependent as the English in their use of balloons – certainly, they used them regularly to save fuel. He wondered idly if the

Americans were in a similar position. They had been the great *'gas guzzlers'* according to his father, though this had been one of the many reasons they had suffered greatly when they had been forced by events to dramatically reduce their energy consumption. With hindsight, they'd done some pretty stupid things; on that both he and his father had agreed. Not least was the seizure of the remaining Alberta tar lands and the clashes with both the Russians and Canadians in the Arctic, and then –unbelievably - more clashes with their traditional allies, the Europeans.

His father had visited New York for a few days with his own parents when Henry had been a child. He'd always told Henry that the Americans were, individually, a warm and caring people, but that – even in his youth- their abilities and ambitions were being perverted by some of the religious crazies with enormous influence in parts of the media and what he had called *'the military industrial complex'*. Henry had remembered that term clearly, and had considered it to be one of his father's originals until he had come across a reference to it on one of the data sites. It seemed that some General called Eisenwoher had developed the term at the end of one of the big wars – at the end of one of the official World Wars if his memory served.

A loud bang, the source of which he failed to identify, shook Henry out of his thoughts. It suddenly occurred to him that, historically, the old United States would have had had no trouble sending their aircraft from the Canaries to bomb bases such as this one at Nuova Lisboa This was one eventuality he did not wish to witness personally. He could not have been alone with such thoughts, for he was relieved to see a number of fighters taxiing out onto the runway, apparently prepared to scramble if required. A small group of trucks also sped past, missiles clearly visible despite the protective tarpaulins.

That way sir, said one of the MPs, and Henry found himself walking into a building, down a long corridor which he felt was leading him deep into the building and then down to a lower level, and finally into a smallish room. The door was closed behind him and Henry heard the distinct sound of a lock shooting into place.

The dimly lit room had doubtless started its existence as a very big room, into which -Henry immediately concluded - had been crammed over time every electronic artefact known to humanity. Evidence for the unplanned, evolutionary nature of these developments was visible in the snaking of cables and wires which spilled everywhere. Some stretched to the ceiling where they disappeared through holes to….? He assumed to another room, with similar machines. *Blame the French. They cannot plan to save their life!* The speaker, a rather over-weight sergeant, had been sitting unseen in the gloom and he gesticulated in the general direction of the disappearing cables. From his accent Henry immediately concluded he was from one of the German lands.

His conclusion was immediately vindicated by a female voice with a strong French touch whose owner had been similarly unseen. *Do not believe the German. They are good at making cable, doing things nice, planning as you say. But wee French have the genius with the computers –these are French machines, made in France.*

Mit technology stolen from the Chinese. We...

You talk too much! A third voice interrupted curtly. *Mr. La Fontaine, I am Lieutenant Madl, 2nd Hungarian Intelligence. I, and these ... buffoons? That is the right English word? We have been ordered to help you. These are the best computers we have access to, and they are linked to intelligence centres throughout Eurocorp. The system is not as fast as it used to be, but we can get the job done. The top officers wants to know what these Americans are doing, why they have occupied these islands – Canaries you call them in English?- and what is going to happen next? I have been told you are an expert in these things. Correct?*

Henry paused before replying. The man's English and pronunciation was probably better than his own and *'It was like the English of what? About twenty or thirty years earlier? Buffoon, when did I hear that used last?'* he asked himself. *Not quite Lieutenant* he finally replied. *I met their president, the crazy one –Smith- at university. I also did some research on him for a qualification I started later.* He hesitated further before deciding that honesty might be an advantage on this occasion. *I understand I have been sent here because more powerful people than me think I may be useful, and may be able to identify what Smith is doing. But this things with the Canaries ....that is a mystery to me. You know of course that they will kill anyone who opposes them? Even saying something negative could be enough. They have this thing about unselected Souls- people not belonging to them- and the fact that they are inferior if they refuse the offer of circumcision and redemption.*

With respect, I suggest we all work to solve this mystery, as you describe it, and find a way of protecting other people from these – you said 'crazy'- ones. I have been informed that, for now, we can give no support to the soldiers on Las Palmas. We have no ships in the area and all flights have been grounded. Another 'bloody' -I think you say?- storm. The weather prediction is that we may be able to fly late this afternoon, and my orders are that you are to produce a coherent prediction of what Smith will do next by 14.00 today.

Really? And how do you propose to do that?
A grim smile crossed Madl's face. *The good news is that I have access to real coffee and real cakes. We four are going to sit and talk. We are going to drag every idea, every crumb –you say so?- of information, every possibility out of your brain and run it through the computers. Not very clever, not very sophisticated, but the best we can do in the time.*
And the bad news?
The good news continues. We will then help you go to home. And the lady who is sleeping with all the officers also – if she wants. I must tell you, this is not a new way of getting information - we have used it before. But she does seem to genuinely like at least a couple of them – especially the Greek one. The bad news is that if we are not successful or... and here Madl's smile faded and something darker came into his face as he paused *or if I feel you are not helping me as much as you can, I have been ordered to throw you out of the camp to find your own way home. A long walk and many long swims, and then the criminals who live outside the Walls...*
Henry blanched. *And the chances of being able to do that would be...?* he dared to ask.
About one percent without the woman. She will attract trouble. I suggest we start working.

33.0 degrees north, 20.1 degrees west
08.19 UTC April 2nd

Lagard's conversation with naval headquarters in Montreal had been highly positive if the desired outcome was to hunt down and sink as many enemy-by which he was given to understand Smith's- vessels as possible. Personally, he considered all Americans enemies. *Yes,* he could proceed at full speed to try and locate the Christian forces. *Yes* he could harry, engage, do anything he wanted to slow, destroy or whatever else he could whilst the Federal American navy made its way east. *Yes* that could take several days, but a vanguard would be sent to join him within forty eight hours. *Yes,* he was disturbed to find that the vanguard was a nuclear submarine– apparently the only functioning one the Federals had in the Atlantic - which, he observed, could destroy *La Cité*. *Yes*, the Federals had offered to open negotiations on the remaining Albertan tars and new Arctic oils in recognition of the great assistance rendered by the Canadian Confederation. There was even some talk of returning what remained of Ontario to Canadian control. *Yes* two more Canadian warships were coming to assist him, but that would be within a week.

He didn't trust the Federal Americans- to deliver, though Lopez had generally proved to be a man of his word in recent negotiations. Lagard had doubts about the security of the navy's encryption, and was about to end what was becoming more than an operational discussion when a sailor literally burst into the room. *Apologies captain. Lieutenant Mullard said that this was of the greatest importance and you needed to read this immediately*! The words were almost shouted, without the slightest trace of respect for rank, and after Lagard had dismissed the man he made the second mental note in as many days to address the issue of onboard discipline. He might bend orders, but his command would not bend his. Opening the envelope, he asked Montreal to stay on line as he skimmed through the message. *Admiral, we have a development here,* he said, returning to Montreal link. *A strange one to my mind. Intel has intercepted a message from the European military. We haven't decrypted it fully yet, but from what we can understand the Americans have landed in the Canary Islands. Any idea why?*

Minutes later, he ordered a change of course and maximum speed. Despite the stabilisers, the three hull sections of his ship started rolling violently to starboard as the new course took *La Cité* side-on to the mounting, northerly waves.

Theoretically, the ship's intelligent systems could adjust for the impact of the sea on its hull. These included adjusting the ballast so that the ship rode deeper in the water, and in extremis each hull could be made water tight and taken down to sea level. The theory had never been fully tested in the open sea, and the vessel was now running high out of the water to maximise its speed. The reduced stability made life uncomfortable for the crew and Lagard feared it would almost certainly reduce the accuracy of his weapons systems. Looking to the north, the near horizon was now a solid sheet of black, with sheet lightning regularly penetrating the gloom. Whilst he wanted to maximise speed, the priority had to be to ensure the structural integrity of the ship and its performance in combat. Consequently, he instructed the chief engineering officer to experiment with changes in the configuration in the hull draughts and to monitor the effect of the changes on speed and stability. These were things which should have be done immediately after the ship had been commissioned nearly six years earlier, but until a few days previously it had effectively been used as a guard-ship at the mouth of the St. Lawrence and had never ventured into the perilous, open Atlantic.

Let's see if we can outrun this, lieutenant. He pointed to the growing storm, and noted the helm officer's growing ting of green.

Second one like this within weeks, she smiled grimly. *No chance of the weekend furlough now I suppose sir?*

Not in Canada lieutenant Lagard laughed. *Perhaps we can have one in Europe instead?*

Chapter V
An Afternoon in Las Palmas
13.08 UTC April 2nd

Adams had spent the morning travelling to, and securing, their position on the north western side of Las Palmas. A series of trenches and hollows had been excavated to provide protection for his troops and their light artillery, and a perimeter established using a couple of M179s captured from the Wuccies in fighting at Richmond. Adams had never seen one of the machines in operation, but they had a terrifying reputation and President Smith himself had ordered that the expedition be provided with the entire stock of ammunition for the weapons. It seemed that there was a problem making replacement bullets, so the guns were to be abandoned along with anything else which slowed their withdrawal.

The weapons had been mounted in such a way that they could sweep over some 220 degrees, though the terrain continued to provide some protection for any potential attacker. The length of his line, straddling some seven miles on the side of the mountain, also meant that it was impossible to provide automated cover for all of the drilling teams. Consequently, in addition to his protected sites, Adams had organized squads of marines in fast armoured half-tracks. These were to move rapidly to support any point under attack. Sadly, Smith had denied him the possibility of any air support, even in extremis, but looking up at the low clouds dashing southwards, he acknowledged once again that the President's foresight was flawless - the weather rendered precision bombing impossible and the success of the mission could easily be jeopardised by inaccurate bombing.

So far, there had been no meaningful resistance, though some of the locals had proved to be a nuisance by taking pot-shots at his men. Their weapons appeared to be simple, single-shot models, though used with considerable skill. One of his marines had been mortally hit in the head, though that had cost the five locals their lives in the subsequent exchange. Now, all was quiet and Adams could concentrate on the task in hand. His early morning had been a time of great anguish. He had not received the pre-arranged instructions to proceed from President Smith until over three hours after the agreed time. Adams would not act without clear instructions, so that delay had already put them behind their schedule.

Then, the incessant rain and increasing wind had slowed their progress up the rough mountain roads-little more than tracks in places- from their landing at Punta towards the Caldera de Taburiente. At one point the road had disappeared totally for a stretch of several hundred yards, and Adams and his senior officers had a heated discussion as to whether to lay a temporary surface over soil blasted from further up the mountain side or to return back, down the mountain and approach from the east. Adams was reluctant to pursue the second alternative, not least because he was unsure how well organized and large the opposition he might encounter would prove. He felt that he was certainly more likely to find greater resistance going back into the lowland than in the unpopulated stretches which lay ahead. In addition, he had studied this island and its geology in detail, both in his unpublished doctoral work and in the months since he had presented his plan to President Smith, God Protect Him. He was therefore confident that he knew enough of the physical characteristics of the land to be confident that it would support tracked vehicles for a short time, especially as the rain appeared to be giving the soil greater viscosity. He gave the order to plant enough charges up the slope to create a new ledge, and the entire column passed without incident.

Now that he had arrived at his destination, he started to consider the additional complexities

arising from his last conversation with President Smith, God Protect Him. The original plan had been to land, establish base, drill and abandon the island before dark. President Smith, *God Protect Him*, had informed Adams that the armada had been slowed
considerably and that there was now a potential 24 hour delay in their schedule. Looking at the clouds and rain, Adams suspected that the armada would be making heavy weather far to the north, but notification of the delay prior to landing would have been invaluable. At sea, they would probably have been safe from enemy intervention. Now that they were on the island, and the enemy knew of their presence, Adams could only speculate as to when, or if, troops would arrive, and in what numbers. Many Souls said that there was no structure or loyalty among the European decadents, in which case he had nothing to concern him, but there was the slightest doubt in the back of his mind.

Work was just starting on six of the eleven shafts- these were the easier, shallower ones. The others would take longer and would either mean moving his troops or leaving some of the drilling teams relatively exposed. After relieving himself in a bush, a marine engineer from the nearest rig jogged towards him, his waterproofs glistening in the rain.

The man smiled. *Permission to speak Christian Brother Captain,* the man said jovially, whilst ensuring that he maintained the full formality of his address.

Permission granted Brother, what can I do for you? Adams replied with a smile. The afternoon was, after all, going well.

I understood we were building missile emplacements, Christian Brother Captain, but I ain't ever seen something like that, he said, gesticulating to the rows of drilling rigs sprouting along the mountain's flank.

That, Brother Captain, is because you engineers have yet to fully learn that the Lord God can move in very mysterious ways. Is that not the case? and the smile disappeared from Adams. The engineer was about to make a jovial reply before the significance of Adams's words struck him. He equaled Adams in rank, but orders were that Adams represented the Commander in Chief himself on this mission. He had simply been intrigued to understand the true nature of their mission, but Adams's reply had touched on the potential for heretical debate and he had no wish to engage in such dangerous talk.

Very true Christian Brother Captain, both the Lord God and our Christian Brother President can move in the most mysterious of ways. And now, with your permission sir, I shall return to my duties. With the most respectful of salutes, he turned and marched swiftly back towards his drilling squad.

Las Palmas

13.17 UTC April 2nd

Anna-Maria lay in a hollow on a brow overlooking the Americans, surrounded by a company of her best troops. The Americans were several kilometres away, but this was both the closest she intended to be and the closest she needed to be. Through her binoculars she could see that the enemy had established a series of defensive positions and she had arrived just in time to witness them assemble two of the weapons she had seen used in Turkey to annihilate the best part of a Eurocorp battalion in less than twenty minutes. The Americans probably knew that she and her men had arrived but seemed fully focused on whatever they were doing. Without highly sophisticated equipment – which she did not have - there was no protection for troops against prying electronic system in the bleak environment which typified their position on the upper slopes of the Caldera de Taburiente. Drones would be the usual tool, but she had nothing which could cope with the wind here.

The American's behaviour worried her. Even here, a decent commander would be doing more to ensure his disposition was concealed and, in addition, the defensive positions which had been constructed were inadequate for the number of men deployed. Most of these, she had already realised were military engineers. There seemed to be little intent to stay in this relatively secure position, which left her lost as to what the objective of this exercise might be. Initially, when the first drilling rig had been erected, she considered they might be constructing a missile base or anti-aircraft site of some sort, but the holes they were drilling appeared to be too deep for foundations and certainly too small for any missile with which she was familiar. For now, she had no option but to wait for the few re-enforcements available from the other islands, and

she ordered a runner to take a message to the communications team she had positioned in a more secure position several hundred meters further down the slope behind her.

Nuova Lisboa

13.58 UTC April 2nd

Henry stood outside the admin building in which he had been entombed until now. He was partly sheltered by the building from the torrential rain, but despite the relative warmth of the rain, he felt a cold sweat breaking out across his body. If the European kept their threat, he and Amanda would be out of the gates in less than fifteen minutes, and would be faced with the nigh-on impossible task of making their own way home. It was a terrifying prospect. Even if they were successful in bribing their way onto some form of transport –*'I wonder how much useful currency we have between the two of us?'* he asked himself- there would almost inevitably be times when they would have to deal with darkness and the great Wetlands. Madl may have been trying to intimidate him with his 1% figure for survival, but, if Henry were totally honest with himself, it would certainly be less than 50-50. Whilst not fully a death sentence, it was a death sentence with a potential for a reprieve.

The day had the potential for being a total disaster. Madl and his team had been quite remarkable, picking up the slightest turn of phrase in Henry's discussion with Smith, his thoughts on Smith's religious beliefs, Henry's analysis of Smith's writings, and so on. The French woman had been particularly skilful, developing a tone of voice which Henry had found totally relaxing, and which she had used to lead Henry back into situations in which he felt he actually was there, sitting next to Smith; retrospectively, he realised that she had hypnotized him. Despite all this, nothing had emerged about the significance of the Canary Islands, and by the time they had finished Henry felt violently ill. They had,

he concluded, put something more than coffee in the cup to assist his memory, and his body was reacting violently to it. Marie-Claire rode rapidly into sight on an ancient bicycle. *'Must care for me, or something, to be out in this'*, he thought to himself. Seeing the look of concern on her face, he decided that perhaps she viewed him as slightly more than a sleeping partner and the worrying thought crossed his mind that he knew nothing about European military regulations and child bearing.
You ok? she asked anxiously, but before Henry could reply Madl crashed through the door. *Ah good,* he addressed both of them. *The more minds the better. The commander on Las Palmas has sent a report that the Americans are drilling deeply on the island. We have only just received the report. Any ideas? Does this President Smith like drilling for some special reason Mr. La Fontaine?*
Henry closed his mouth before the word *'No.'* could issue from it. It was nothing that Smith had ever talked about, but he had a vague memory of reading something, somewhere, many years ago about the geography –or was it the geology?- of the Canaries and…. *Just had an idea. Can we go inside and use your computers. Maybe I can explain what is going on after all, though you didn't need an expert on Smith for this.*
You mean you are expendable? Madl replied with a broad grin.

No, I mean that I may be the genius who has solved our riddle and earned himself a safe passage home, Henry replied warmly, failing to notice the anguish which passed across Marie-Claire's face.

34.8 degrees north, 17.8 degrees west
17.59 UTC April 2nd

The day had been a major disaster for Smith, and he was having difficulty finding someone to blame. His overnight whim had substantially slowed the progress of the armada; he had forgotten to contact Adams to delay his landing in the light of their new delay, and now God was punishing him with yet another storm. This time he had been obliged to instruct Monroe to order all ships to lower their sails and use their precious fuel reserves to maintain maximum speed. Monroe had soon persuaded him to rescind the latter order. The smaller vessels were struggling to cope with ten metre tall waves washing over their port sides, and across the armada reports were coming in of people being injured, cargo breaking away, and the occasional fatalities. Towards the end of the afternoon the *Morning Star's* engines had failed and the ships had wallowed helplessly in the mountainous swell before plunging broadside on into a trough between the waves. Rocking wildly, the ship had been caught almost immediately by another large wave and turned turtle. The ship's hatches had been sealed against the storm, the air inside keeping a large part of the hull clear of the water.

In other circumstances the ship could have been righted or an escape hole been cut in the hull to rescue survivors – there were desperate radio pleas from those entombed in the hulk. In current circumstances there was nothing Monroe was prepared to risk for the hundred or so Souls and crew. He had immediately decided that he would not endanger another vessel by attempting any form of rescue- and endanger the entire fleet if they did not continue to make good speed. The *Morning Star* was still afloat when the last of the armada left it drifting far astern. Smith reacted to events by flying into another of his hysterical depressions in which he alternated doubt if The Lord still favoured him with racking his brain for a potential cause of this ill fortunate.

Monroe could no longer suppress his serious doubts about Smith's continued stability, and was increasingly convinced that, should the opportunity arise, Smith would slip back several hundred years and cast about for witches and wizards as potential causes of his troubles. The President had already regressed into a repeated, heavy reliance on his own Inquisition to root out heretical traitors to the cause, though Monroe suspected that his current behaviour arose in part from a conscious or subconscious knowledge that his actions and omissions had created some of their current difficulties. For now, Smith was in communion with the Lord in his cabin and Monroe was left in peace to command. The next difficulty would be informing Smith that it was now impossible to achieve their objective as scheduled, and he found himself pondering the implications of this for Adams and his command.

31.8 degrees north, 19.2 degrees west
19.58 UTC April 2nd

Lagard had been elated by *La Cité's* performance. Some clever guesstimates and experimentation had established what appeared to be an excellent configuration to cope with current sea conditions. Life on board ship had also become easier when they shifted to a more southerly course, resulting in less lateral roll and an increase in their speed. Lagard remained apprehensive as to how the ship would behave if it were hit directly astern by one of the larger waves, though experience thus far had been that the craft had exceeded all her design specifications. Now, he was cutting his speed and trying to find a profile in the water which would enable his crew to get a good night's sleep.

It had taken some considerable time, and heated discussion, for Montreal to decide that he should proceed south to the Canaries and identify the intent of the Christian Americans. La Cité was probably the best ship in the Eastern Canadian Fleet, and its loss would leave the eastern seaboard more vulnerable to attack. Lagard sensed that the Federal Americans had promised to reward Canada for its assistance and worried that this might be at the expense of his ship and crew. While he had no idea of the size or capability of the force he was about to encounter, he felt somewhat reassured by the designer's claims that his vessel could almost certainly out-run anything the Christians had. Irritatingly, the reality that there was no prospect of out-running their missiles also continuously crept into his mind.

Short of being detected and sunk, at worst he could simple observe serrupticiously and report. But to whom? At best, he could engage in some hit-and-run and that had become even more interesting after he received a range of frequencies and encryption details enabling him to contact the regional European naval headquarters in Madrid. In the old days it would have been a simple satellite call, but given the increasing unreliability of the old *'birds'* as he remembered them being called, the use of short-wave frequencies had been re-established. Looking at his frequency list, Lagard doubted some would work at this distance, but the addition of another actor gave him a further sense that something truly significant was in progress. For the European and Americans to cooperate after the conflicts of recent years? Well, his father had once told him that everything came full circle with enough time.

If all had gone well, they would have reached Las Palmas during the night, but he had no desire to meet the enemy with a tired crew and in such turbulent seas. It worried him deeply that many of the crew had no battle experience and that even their practice of battle conditions had been severely limited by budget cuts. *'Rather like asking an unlicensed eighteen year old to drive a sports car,'* Lagard mulled to himself, though it then occurred to him that some of the youngest crew members would have little inkling of the potential of the old sports cars and the only licences they might hold would almost certainly be to drive military vehicles or public transports.

Everything in order ? he enquired. The deck duty officer was the same one as had been gently lamenting the loss of her leave furlough that morning. Now, she looked even greener.

Yes captain, she replied through gritted teeth, *though I've not enjoyed these seas. I couldn't really sleep when I was off duty. The St. Lawrence is a pond compared to this. Is this normal out here?*

Normal? What is normal lieutenant Polawski? Lagard laughed. *I haven't seen normal for over twenty years. If you find it, you have my permission to capture it. However, if you are satisfied that all is in order, I am going to do something very normal – get some good sleep. When you are relieved at midnight, I want you make sure that you order the next shift officer to wake me at 05.00. And you, Lieutenant,* he said turning to the duty tactics officer sitting behind another console, *I want you to ensure that you keep a close eye on the radar and electronic warfare systems. I want all systems and crew taken to the next alert level from 03.00 - earlier if you identify anything suspicious. That order is clear? Again, you are to communicate it to your relief. Understood?*

Yes sir! he replied.

'Probably just turned twenty one,' Lagard thought to himself and, shooting both officers a smile, he left the bridge for the relative comfort of his cabin.

Nuova Lisboa

20.00 UTC April 2nd

Henry, Marie-Claire and Amanda sat in a glum huddle at one end of the officers' mess. It was a pleasantly functional building, well-lit and furnished with some beautiful plants. Henry could not identify them, but their glorious red flowers produced a delightful, relaxing perfume. Regardless of the quality of the building, the rain drumming constantly on the roof, and the wind howling outside, were vivid reminders that nothing would be flying out of any of the bases in the area until the storm had abated. This was a critical problem in the light of their discussions earlier in the evening.

Madl and his team had gone to find someone who would still make them something substantial to eat. It was early by traditional southern European standards, but even here the day had been truncated by energy shortages. The solar and PV panels were fine for lighting and even basic energy supply, but cooking was very energy demanding and demands for greater efficiency had limited cooking to shorter periods earlier in the day. They soon returned with something that had a smell akin to coffee and the promise that '*a proper meal*' of fish and potatoes would be following within the half hour. *Don't all look so sad!* Madl chirped as he approached, though his smile betrayed an inner tension.

Talk for yourself! Amanda snapped. *I reckon I was happier before Henry came up with his bloody explanation. This is really horrible. If he is right, we should start doing something now, and I mean now. And if he's wrong, we are going to cause panic and chaos for nothing.*

What your friend enry said.. Marie-Claire started, before Amanda corrected her with *What my colleague said sweetie. He's all yours.* Marie-Claire smiled before starting again with a calculated deliberation clearly intended to irritate. *Like I was starting to say, your friend enry may be wrong, but it is a good*

explanation. What do you think they will do now Lieutenant Madl?

Madl kept his head low as though he had developed a profound interest in the contents of his cup. Then, when he lifted his head, his face uncharacteristically revealed that he was struggling with his emotions. *Not the stuff of a hardened intelligence officer this lieutenant,* Henry quipped. Marie-Claire's vicious kick made him instantly recognise his stupidity.

True Mr. La Fontaine, but even we 'tough guys' have out limits. And I'm not professional military, just someone doing his –what do you call it? Conscription time I think. I was teaching maths and software design in Budapest until they called me, and apparently I am very good at the thinking they need for intelligence work ...so here I am. And you?

Sweeties, can we stick to the point? Amanda interjected. Henry immediately understood she was fearful the conversation could drift to where she did not want it to go. *Not that I would like anyone to think I supported her,* and she inclined her head towards Marie-Claire. *What the fuck do you think is going to be done?*

Madl looked around. The room was empty though there were noises come from the chefs in the

kitchen and a growing, appealing aroma. *I do not know,* he confided reluctantly. *You could all see how shocked the top commanders were with what Henry –I can call you that, ok?- was suggesting. Now they will discuss it, and if they believe what he has said they will report it to headquarters. I think they will do this even if they have doubts – it is too important to be left at this level. Then the government will try to decide what damage will be caused, and to whom, if this man Smith is successful. I think you must remember that things have not been good between America and Europe for many years now – we are not at war, but....*
But effectively we have been, added Marie-Claire. *Which is also why they may deciding what to say to your government,* and she looked directly into Henry and Amanda's faces. *You have American Federal military on your territory. That is seen as a potential threat, and some of them were involved in combat against our forces. I think you must be realistic – we do not have to help you and it may be in our interests to see you further damaged.*
But we have been helping you! Amanda shouted across the table. *And it was Henry here who offered an explanation for Smith behaviour. Without him much of the European coast would be sitting innocently waiting to die!!*
Only much? Only European? Madl interjected. That may be very – optimistic as you say in English. *Ah good! Food is ready. And for now, we can do nothing. This Smith is being protected by the weather – perhaps he is right*

and the God is really with him. Tonight he is certainly not with us – we cannot even move some armoured vehicles from their shelters in case they are damaged. And further south? Henry enquired after a cook had carefully placed a steaming plate in front of him.

Further south we have two base near the old Spanish – Portuguese frontier. They are in the hills north of the Cadiz-Jerez marshes. Marie-Claire volunteered instantly, despite a warning glance from Madl. *They have some aircraft, but mostly marines and coastal batteries to protect against raiders from the south – the Moroccan Caliphate I think you say in Engleesh. I heard the weather reports from that area earlier this afternoon. It is perhaps worser even than here. No... worse than here. I must be tired, my English is not so good this evening.*

Better than his French bun, despite the fancy name, Amanda volunteered. *But let's eat before it gets cold. Lovely Lieutenant Madl, does your influence extend as far as some fine white wine to go with this? Eat drink and be merry, for tomorrow we may die! Right? And I might be able to reward you later,* she added with the broadest of smiles. Henry and Marie-Claire shot each other a glance and struggled to control their laughter. *My influence may extend to the wine,* Madl replied dryly *but haven't you already rewarded almost all the officers? But I do have a male dog.*

Amanda sat stony face throughout the rest of the meal, shoving her food into her mouth as rapidly as she could and refusing to touch the wine Madl had obtained. As soon as she had finished, she stormed off, and after a short while Madl and his team followed. *It was not easy getting information from im,* Marie-Clair volunteered as they left but then he did not know so much. He is just lucky. Giggling violently, the trio declared

themselves to be totally exhausted and headed for bed.

Left alone, Henry could feel a novel tension between himself and Marie-Claire. It wasn't like the first few days which had been characterised by a mixture of hostility and intrigue. This was different, and after a considerable silence Marie-Claire came to the point. *You ave a wife and child in London,* she blurted out in a mixture of statement and accusation.

Henry hesitated. *Yes I do. I know I should have told you, but .....*

But you thought you would have some fun with me? Mmmm, I think I was stupid. I should have known – you are too pretty to have escaped the women for long. I was stupid also because you are an agent of a foreign government. And we are not friendly with it.

That is causing you problems?

No, my commander was quite pleased we slept together. He thinks it was a good way to get information from you. Now, it seems your knowledge of Smith was not useful, but the fact that you had read an old geographique magazine was. That was lucky.

So now you don't have to sleep with me? Henry replied sharply, though his face betrayed another emotion.

That is the problem. I don't need an order to sleep with you more. You are a bastard in some ways, but in other ways I like you very much and...

Thank you, I feel the same –though I think you are a bit of a bitch rather than a bastard, he interrupted with a broad grin, and he held his hand out to her.

No, I need to think about what I am doing now, she replied, and moved her hand away. *But I like you enough to do one more stupid thing.*

Henry's heart sank. '*Please no, I haven't got her pregnant have I?*' he demanded inwardly. *And what is that may I ask?* he enquired hesitantly.

If you are right Monsieur La Fontaine, your wife and baby are in great danger if they are in the flat lands. Amanda – she appears to care for no one. But I have a feeling that you do care for your family. I am right? Henry nodded, unsure as to what was coming. *I have permission for you to make once telephone call-maximum two minutes. I can only be to your wife, and it must be in simple Engleesh so that I can understand. You know the geography of your country –*

so if you love her you will say her to go somewhere safe. This is only to your wife, you will not call your government and you will not say anything which could be a code. You understand?
Marie-Claire, that is so kind of you. I am so grateful, Henry found himself saying with a genuine intensity. No one could claim he was a man of great depth in his sentiments, but on this occasion he was genuinely surprised by his feelings. *And if I make a mistake or am a naughty boy?* his alter ego demanded.
I said I liked you, Marie-Claire retorted with a new coldness. *But remember I am an officer who loves her job, country and Europe. If you are, as you say, a naughty boy,* she said with a half smile but indicating her regulation sidearm, *I shall shoot out any brains you ave in your head.*

Las Palmas
23.25 UTC April 2nd

Adams was awoken from a fitful slumber in the back of an armoured half-tracks by the opening of the rear hatch. Instantly, the howling of the wind was more evident, a few drops of rain being swept into the relative warmth and dry, and then a figure clambered in and closed the door. Adams could hear the sound of a hand groping for a light switch in the darkness. The weather was causing major problems with the infrared and other security, and 'the enemy', which was whoever was causing them grief on the island, had taken advantage of this to come within firing range. Not that the weather had been of any help to them, and the shots appeared to either have been fired by amateurs or swept off target by the power of the winds. It was, however, enough to encourage heads to be kept down and to make drilling proceed less effectively. Even the armoured vehicles were trembling slightly in the wind, and Adams had ordered that they be weighed down with any spare junk to maximize stability. *Who's there?* he demanded anxiously, the thought suddenly occurring to him that he was unsure as to whether the figure he had briefly glimpsed was a friend or foe.

Me sir, said a voice less then helpfully, though this coincided with the light switch being found. It was the same officer he had spoken to earlier in the day, though now he was covered from head to foot in filth and water was pouring down his waterproofs. *Christian Brother, Sir,* he continued, and Adams immediately sensed bad news. He had seen how this formality was always used with *Christian President Smith* when officers wished to break bad news- even Admiral Monroe tended to do the same. *We have had to stop drilling,* and the man stopped to see how Adams reacted.

Why? Adams demanded, though he suspected that

he already knew the reason.

The wind is destroying the rigs Christian Brother. One has already been blown over and twisted and another has buckled the drill itself and…

So you've ordered the drilling halted? And the rigs taken down? Adams demanded, sitting bolt upright in the cramped confines of the troop carrier.

Yes Sir, the officer replied apprehensively.

Good man! Adams exclaimed, and he could almost feel the tension drain from the other man. *We cannot work when The Lord does not will it. We can finish this work in the morning when the weather improves. Tell your men to get some rest. Have you thought that this could be a message? It may be difficult here, but I am sure that Our Lord will be using this storm to inflict terrible damage on any Wuccies who have dared to try and follow us.*

And our own fleet, will… was the start of an incautious sentence.

Our fleet, Adams said with considerable emphasis, *is the fleet of Our Lord. He will protect it from evil. You can be sure of this –are you not?*

I certainly am Christian Brother Sir. His emphasis indicated again an awareness of straying into dangerous, theological territory.

Good, then go and get some sleep. Be prepared to start work again at dawn. But for now, please be so kind as to send me the marine commander. We need to do something about our friends.

After the man had left, Adams lay back in the darkness. What he had said was not totally accurate. The damage to the drills would give him an excuse to delay departure for perhaps another day, and that time would hopefully give the main armada time to reach their next objective. He could only assume that President Smith was encountering similar weather and that this was the reason for the armada's delay

Las Palmas

23.30 UTC April 2nd

Anna-Maria lay in the torrential rain on a series of mouldy, wooden planks which her men had ripped from a decaying observation point further down the mountain. She could hear, and almost feel, the water pouring down the small gulley beneath, though so far she had been pleasantly surprised by the quality of the Eurocorp issue waterproofs. She was still dry, and her spirits had been much improved by a cup of hot chocolate brewed at the rear camp and brought up in a flask by her runner. She feared radio communications would definitely give her position away, and her experience was that low technology was always best with the American, regardless of their religious persuasion.

There was no possibility of reinforcements reaching

her now in the storm, and what she had observed was convincing proof that she was in no position, either numerically or in terms of equipment, to take-on the marines. Her orders until now were simply to observe and to harass, but she was less than convinced that the Americans would leave her untouched when conditions improved. For now, she was intrigued to observe a series of quick flashes of light on the left side of the very large gulley which separated her from the Americans. *The command centre?* she mused, though she was unsure as to what use she could make of this information.

LondonWall

00.29 UTC April 3rd

Rachel La Fontaine swore vehemently at the phone's first shrill. John had been ill all day and she had only recently managed to get him to sleep before falling asleep herself on the sofa. She didn't feel so well either. *'How many weeks over am I now?'* she asked herself, and again cursed her irresponsibility in not taking extra precautions after throwing-up during a heavy drinking session with Henry. She hadn't had a chance to talk to him before he had been taken away, and with every day that passed she was growing increasingly aware that she had to make a decision – with or without Henry. True, they had talked about having another one, but with his current wage and rations…?

Hello, who is this? And why are you calling at this bludy time? she demanded down the line.

Rache, it's me Henry, came a thin voice. The quality of the line was appalling and she had to strain to catch the words.

Henry! she shouted, surprised by the depth of feelings his voice aroused. *Where are you? When are you coming home? What's happening? I've…*

Stop, please Rachel luv, I'm on limited time. U luv me? Yes?

Corse I do, she replied, though she could have sworn she heard a female tittering in the background. *Why do you ask?*

Listen carefully, I want you to take the first transport out of London tomorrow. The very first, I'm..

I can't do that, Rachel replied indignantly, *John is ill and I've managed to get an appointment for him with a doctor tomorrow afternoon, I can't…*

Bloody listen woman! Henry shouted with such vehemence that it caused the ear piece to hiss *Get out of London – if you don't you may both be dead within days and ..*

Forty five seconds passed, observed a foreign female in the background.

Who's that with you Hen? Rachel demanded, a surge of jealousy distracting her from the original conversation.

No one important. Just listen, he replied with growing urgency. *You must get out – it's vital. Tell no one. Listen, I have a sister in the Sheffield SafeLands. Her name is Lucy. She will help you. Tell her that you are Bart's wife and that she must remember how weak the Walls are. You got that? I…*

What the hell are you talking about Henry? You never told me you had a sister. What's her name? And since when were you Bart? Have you gone mad or summit? Rachel retorted.

One minute and fifteen seconds passed, said the foreign female in the background.

Please listen, write down this number and do as I say. I'll explain everything when I get back. There was growing desperation in his voice.

OK, give me the bloody number and I'll ring this Lucy girl, Rachel replied apprehensively. This was not the normal behavior of her man. *But it'll be after I've taken John to the doc,* she added firmly, her maternal instincts rising to the surface. *But what's going on?*

Take the number dam it, and do as I say! Henry shouted

One minute and forty five seconds said the same voice.

He barely had time to gabble out the number when the base operator replaced the countdown with a simple *Ligne coupé pour des raisons de sécurité*

Nuoava Lisboa
00.31 UTC April 3rd

Shit, fuck, shit! Henry screeched in the small booth into which he and Marie-Claire had both crammed. He had wanted her to stay outside, but she had insisted that he was more likely to be disturbed if she was seen hanging around outside.

No good? Marie-Claire enquired hesitantly, somewhat taken aback by this new, aggressive Henry's.

The stupid, stupid woman wouldn't listen. I need to ring her back. Please, only another minute. Can't you get permission for another minute? By this time they had tumbled, rather than stepped, out of the booth into the dimly lit corridor. A fat, ageing sergeant sat near what appeared to be the main switchboard, his interest clearly aroused by the shouting.

No, no more time, Marie-Claire said grimly. *There was no permission to call. I had to get im,* and she inclined her head towards the sergeant *to let you make the call. And now I ave to fuck im as his reward, or he will report us both. So no more calls. Just go now.*

Chapter VI
Towards The Pillars of Hercules
29. 8 degrees north, 19.4 degrees west
05.36 UTC April 3rd

Confusion was the word to epitomise La Cité's crowded battle room. Having raced across the Atlantic in pursuit of a fleet consisting of perhaps hundreds, perhaps a thousand enemy vessels– intelligence was no longer a military strong point-*La Cité du Québec's* drone had located a squadron of exactly fifteen ships anchored off the coast of Las Palmas. True, there a couple of prime targets, front line warships, but the majority were armed transports which were riding so high in the water that they must have unloaded whatever they had been carrying. These were not, however, the mass of mixed military and civilian vessels which Lagard had expected to encounter, and amongst which he had hoped his great speed and manoeuvrability would enable him to generate sufficient havoc to avoid his own destruction. True, an attack on this purely military formation might result in damage to one or two ships, but *La Cité's* destruction would be assured. So what had gone wrong?

Could be that this is a detachment and that the main fleet has rounded the islands and on their way to the African coast, ventured Singh. As the senior intelligence officer there was a great responsibility on his shoulders, but the next words revealed much. *Not that I'd put a buck of my rations on it. I'm just guessing.*

I haven't been paid for nearly three months now, observed Mullard, *so your bet is pretty empty Dav, unless you are doing better than the rest.*

An immediate ripple of tension-alleviating laughter swept the room, before Lagard's crisp voice cut it dead. *So suggestions as to what to do? If you please ladies and gentlemen. We've missed a furlough chasing these crazies across the ocean and I'm not wishing to go home empty handed. I want a few scalps. They owe it us,* he ended bitterly. Most officers of the crew knew that the screams of the dying and wounded on the *Halifax* still haunted him many nights.

With respect captain, I think discretion is better than bravery in this situation,

Mullard almost mumbled, his bowed head reflecting the anguish and reluctance he felt. *I suggest we withdraw out of their Intel range –or at least our best guess on that – and communicate what we have found. Could be the Europeans or Fed Yanks could use the info. And don't they have a sub on its way ahead of the main battle fleet? Could be we should all be looking somewhere else. Can't see what they would do in Africa except fight with the Chinese*

or their Nigerian friends. Taking on the Chinese down here is definitely not a good idea- as they found last time.
I agree captain, Singh added instantly. Something is wrong here. *These Christians have nothing to do with this part of the world – I don't even think they know much about it from their preaching. Or am I wrong? It's the wrong place for these people. We have missed something – a clue- somewhere.*
Lagard hesitated. Finally he shook his head wearily. *OK, it makes sense. 100 miles should take us out of their range and allow us to contact whoever is around from our team – if I can call it that. All we've done so far is follow an old lead from the Europeans, so things may have changed since then. But we wait for the drone to come home. We've only got one other and I don't see a budget for more. Agreed?*

LondonWall

10.41 UTC April 3rd

Rachel la Fontaine wheeled her son out of the relative peace of the doctor's office and onto the crowded pavement. There was a WorkExchange at the end of the road and the pavement was full of jostling people still queuing in the hope of exchanging their labour for some food, shelter or whatever else might be offered. It was long past the time when anyone at this point in the queue had even the remotest chance of getting any work, but – in the absence of anything else to do, and in the presence of desperation- most would stay there all day. Behind the thin screen of assistant police dressed in dark blue uniforms a couple of vans full of squads of riot police were parked on the corner, the silver of their body armour reflecting distinctly in the sunlight entering the vans. There were often small riots when people became truly desperate, but this was unlikely so close to the start of the month when everyone had received at least their basic rations. Today should be peaceful.

John normally walked the distance they had covered, but felt so ill that she had used his old chair to push him to the surgery. The doctor had diagnosed a high fever and recommended bed for at least the next two days. She'd sold Rachel some good quality – so she said- antibiotics, one which he claimed were the latest development and would work against viruses and bacteria. Henry wouldn't have approved, he was sceptical of such claims, but Henry was – '*Well, exactly where is he?*' Rachel asked herself. She had tried getting a straight answer from his work, but all they would say was that he was cooperating with the Euro military on a matter of national importance and would be back when he was back. Rounding the corner she thought back to the bizarre conversation she had had last night. '*Had he drunk too much?*' she asked herself, '*And what was it with the name and sudden development of a sister?' Well I'm damned if I'm taking John anywhere in this state!* she found herself declaring to the surprise of a passing woman, though she made a mental note to try the number later in the day if John were asleep and she could get a line.

35.7 degrees north, 16.8 degrees west
11.21 UTC April 3rd

Smith and Monroe stood together on the bridge of *Genesis*, almost their home now, their proximity signalling the combined stress felt by both men. The sky to the north was showing some signs of clearing, but the waves and wind continued to harry them as though they were agents for the heathen Wuccies. Inwardly, Monroe was cursing himself for not having taken a more direct route. That would have shortened their journey by a day or two, and would not have resulted in their sailing into the wind and waves for what now felt like an eternity. He had long since ceased listening to pleas to *slow*, or try a slight change in tack which would reduce the misery of the Souls crammed below deck. Perhaps inevitably, given the weather, he had lost another three small vessels and now the first urgent calls were coming in from ships whose fuel reserves were running low. On the former his conscience was clear.

He had urged Smith not to take some of these

smaller craft, convinced that they would have struggled even in the old days and would likely fail in the storms which now regularly wreaked havoc across the seas. For now, the growing disorder in the fleet was at least partly to their advantage. Monroe calculated that they still had well over four hundred vessels of various sizes and capabilities, and all of these had to be funneled through a channel some fourteen miles wide in the shortest possible time.

He had finally heard from Adams that the drilling had been slowed by technical problems, a clear *GodSent* given that he was falling further and further behind the original schedule. Adams was also still very much in the centre of the storm, though the improving conditions Monroe was experiencing suggested that the better weather would reach him late that afternoon. In the meantime, Monroe had ordered that Adams dispatch any surplus vessels to rejoin the main fleet at the earliest opportunity.

Another *GodSent* was the weather itself. Smith had informed Monroe that, in this as in many things, Adams had been proved correct in predicting that the Europeans would have effectively abandoned remote locations such as the Canaries. True, there had been contact with enemy forces but these were so lightly armed, and in such tiny numbers, that they posed no threat to his operations. However, by now the European governments would know of their incursion and might be considering sending reinforcements. Now that the entire timetable had slipped, his growing concern was that the main fleet might encounter any forces being sent to aid the Canaries. He had no doubt that his capital ships would be able to match anything the Europeans might send, but his concern was the vulnerability of the majority, which were no more than modified civilian vessels. The bad weather would likely keep any such threat from the European either in harbour or grounded, and every passing hour reduced the prospects of meeting organised resistance on the western side of the passage. Having come to understand Smith's plans more fully, he felt more assured of their relative safety once the channel had been navigated.

Las Palmas

11.42 UTC April 3rd

Anna-Maria's companies had dug in during the night so that they could lay down at least a light, repressive fire on the American positions. She had been seriously considering withdrawing to the safety of the valley until she had received orders in the early hours to hold the ridge at all costs and to delay the drilling. The order was from the Commander-in-Chief himself, and though a full explanation was not forthcoming on the weak radio link, it was impressed on her that the order was to hold the position to the last soldier. *The safety of Europe depends on it,* had been the rather mysterious and unhelpful observation, though the promise of substantial reinforcements once the weather improved had initially been enough to raise morale. Indeed, a boat had set off early that morning from one of the nearby islands with a platoon of paramilitary police on board, though it had been forced to turn back once it had lost the protection of the land and entered open sea.

Now, the Americans were taking advantage of the improved weather to move their own troops forward. They had taken some casualties but were increasingly pinning down her own troops. Regardless of orders, there was no logic in seeing her command massacred when they were no longer able to even see what the Americans were doing. For now, her units still command the gulley up which she and her troops had initially come, and she ordered her troops to withdraw down this. She remained with the rearguard to maximize covering fire during the retreat.

30.2 degrees north, 19.6 degrees west
19.22 UTC April 3rd

The watch was still doubled, but Lagard had stood down most of the crew during the afternoon. They had spent much of the night and all of the morning at battle stations, and in the absence of instructions and clarification from home he had decided that they had done all that was humanly possible. Some had headed directly to their bunks after eating, whilst others had crammed into the rear of the mess to view one of the old classics. Lagard liked the film, some entertaining stuff about time travel called *Back to the Future,* and had decided to stay with the crew to watch it for the ninth or tenth time in a couple of years.

He'd only seen about the first hour and was getting to the point when things got really exciting -in his opinion- when the Duty Officer had rung him. He'd taken the call from Montreal on a secure line, and now found himself looking over the rails at the stern of La Cité. It was pouring with rain and the swell and roll of the ship was such that he shouldn't really have been on deck, but the conversation had left him in a cold sweat. It seemed that the Europeans had come up with a potential explanation as to Smith's plans. If they were right .... well, if they were right the potential damage to Canada was greater even than that inflicted during the Northern Energy Wars. Certainly the Federal Americans were taking it sufficiently seriously to consider ordering an evacuation from parts of the eastern seaboard. After the conversation with Montreal, he'd been patched into a conversation with Admiral Torgut himself, the bastard who had defeated the Canadian Arctic Squadron during Lagard's first posting.

According to Torgut, the majority of his Atlantic Fleet was only four hundred miles to Lagard's north west and was making good time, though Lagard suspected that it would inevitably run into the rear of his storm and would be slowed. The chilling thought occurred to him that his sole, Canadian warship was going to be a sandwich filling between several hundred American ships, each of which would normally be considered hostile. For now, naval headquarters had ordered him to place La Cité under Torgut's command, and after an initially frosty discussion the two men had agreed that the ship's location and speed meant it was admirably placed to try and locate the main Christian formation. Based on intelligence trickling in from the Europeans, Torgut was convinced that they were heading for the Mediterranean. He had a pet theory that Monroe's extreme fundamentalism might cause him to try and join forces with one of the extreme religious groups which had emerged following the region's own conflict between liberals and fundamentalists.

Given their location, Torgut saw Smith's force as more an immediate threat to the Europeans, but Lopez had ordered the attack on WashingtonWall be revenged. It was made clear to Lagard that Washington would be '*...extremely grateful for any hindrance which could delay Monroe ...*'. and his help in establishing their precise location might also remove the necessity to slow for refuelling. Contradicting what he had earlier said, Torgut had also made it clear to Lagard that he wanted first blood against the Christian fleet. The wireless link had broken at that juncture and Lagard wryly observed to Mullard that first blood usually went to first finder.

Through the wind and sea were calming, the course ordered by Torgut would again tend to expose La Cité to the worst of the stormy sea. Disregarding his orders, Lagard decided to reduce vessel's rolling by taking a more northerly route and reducing speed before steering directly east later that night. For now, his first priority was to ensure that his crew had a good night's rest before they started their new chase. Few had slept well in the storms of the last days, and though he might have to obey orders from the Americans he would do so on his terms. Despite the assurances from Montreal, he dreaded the prospect of finding himself in close range of either American faction.

Las Palmas

19.22 UTC April 1st

God had been good to Captain John Matthew Adams, or certainly that was his current feeling. The rain and winds had abated sufficiently to allow him to finish the drilling, his marines had forced the European down the mountains so that they could no longer harry his men, and now he was preparing to leave to join the main fleet. The final shaft was fast being capped with concrete to a thickness which would prevent the Europeans from drilling or blasting their way through to the pods deposited at the base of the shaft. True, they would not resist indefinitely, but long enough for his mission to be achieved. His artifers were busy mining the perimeter from which his teams were now silently withdrawing, and the first companies had already reached the landing crafts which were ferrying them out to his waiting ships. The weather was slowing the operation, but Adams had managed to identify a sheltered stretch on the coast from an old satellite photo, and God was helping with the wind and waves.

He had carefully selected the vessel to use on the

mission, and with President Smith's agreement had identified those which best combined speed and military capability. Four of these now remained, the others having been scuttled. It was a great loss to destroy the ships, but their cargoes remained ashore and their demands on fuel and limited speeds rendered them a liability in the mission ahead. With hindsight Adams wondered why he had bothered to sink the vessels- their fate was already sealed.

As soon as they had taken their full contingent aboard, his remaining squadron had been ordered to sail at maximum speed and rendezvous at Sidi Ifni on the coast of what had been Morocco. There was no intelligence on the state of the government or non-government in the area, and doubtless there were dangers in a land journey cutting the corner through the Moroccan mountains and meeting up with Admiral Monroe on the Mediterranean coast, but Adams calculated that they had the weaponry and transport to make such an objective attainable – God Willing. Another hour and the rearguard would be onboard and their race to safety would begin.

LondonWall

02.50 UTC April 2nd

John had finally fallen asleep. Rachel had given him the antibiotics as soon as they'd arrived home, and he had promptly projectile vomited them, and his stomach's contents, across the sofa. Natasha, a nurse friend, had dropped around later in the day, taken one doubtful look at the packet of medicine, and shot back to her hospital *To get some real stuff, not the crap you've been sold.* She'd returned an hour later and '*the real stuff*' did seem to be helping. Now Natasha had gone, after finishing the last of what had been really RealCoffee, and helping Rachel to finish two bottles of good wine from what Henry called his *cellar.* How a cupboard under the sink could be called a cellar was a mystery to Rachel.

Sitting on the best armchair – she would have preferred lying on the sofa but it stank from John's vomit- she found herself thinking about the previous evening's bizarre telephone conversation. She was sure there was a woman with him- not that was unusual- and her instincts told her that this was probably another of the females Henry had a tendency to pick up, sleep with, and drop. Not that Rachel approved, but Henry was a great catch as a husband. He combined a degree of status, income, an entire flat, and enough attention and care to leave Rachel feeling that he probably wouldn't leave her in the foreseeable future. And she did love him – didn't she? Well, at least a bit, or even more than a bit if he would stop being such a bastard. But this thing about the name and calling what Rachel thought of as an *'instant family'–* well, that was something different.

Looking at her watch, her sober side realized that it was far too late to call anyone then, but the drunken side dominated and she suddenly realized that she was waiting for a reply from the number she had dialed. It was so late that almost everyone would be in bed, all but essential power costing a fortune at this time. Consequently, the lines were magically clear, though there was no reply from the other end. Eventually, a crackly answer machine started, and a male voice gave a name and proclaimed a range of work skills which the owner was clearly keen to impress as lying within his repertoire of skills. In her drunker state the best that Rachel could do was leave a garbled and deeply embarrassed message asking Bart's, Henry's, whoever's, sister to contact her; but in a sudden burst of clarity before she put the handset down, she remembered to add *And he said to remember the weak Wall.*

She was woken from a drunken sleep still in the armchair. Her head hurt incredibly – the best wine was perhaps not so good- and her neck was cramped from having slept in a poor position. She scrabbled around for the handset in the semi-darkness, desperately hoping that she would find it before it woke John. Noting from the wall clock that it was almost three in the morning, she assumed it would be Henry and that it would be one of his sporadic drunken calls. He had always done that from time to time when he was away on what he called business and was feeling guilty. *Why the hell are you calling at this bloody time? One of your women kicked you out?* she barked, instantly regretting both the exertion which increased the searing pain in her head and the hostility in her voice. He had, after all, rung.

There was a silence for several seconds, though Rachel could sense there was someone at the other end. *Who are you?* a woman's voice finally demanded at the other end. *You left a message on my husband's phone. I've just been to the toilet and picked it up. Why were you calling so late?* There was something powerfully territorial and defensive in the tone, and Rachel instantly sensed that this was another woman trying to hang on to an errant partner. Her immediate instinct was to hang up, but instead she blurted out *Are you Bart's sister? Bart told me to ring you.*

Bart been dead for years, the voice lied curtly. Territorial perhaps, but an honest person not accustomed to lying. So Rachel surmised. *Anyway, what you want?*

I'm not sure Rachel replied hesitantly. *My husband suddenly told me that he has been lying about his name for years, and told me that he has a sister called Lucie. He gave me this number to ring and said I should talk to Lucie.*

And this Bart is your husband? Why can't he ring himself?

Working for the government- with the Europeans, Rachel replied, her voice betraying the importance she felt such information deserved, but doubtful that she should be revealing such things to a total stranger. She was pleased to hear the slightest gasp of surprise from the other end, though even more surprised at the response. *Still with McGregor? Or does he have a new post?* Trying to clear her head from the alcohol, Rachel realized that it was the European part which had been the surprise for the speaker.

So you two have been in contact? she demanded. *And your link is?*

There was a long pause and this time she heard a male voice in the background, clearly asking what was happening. *I don't know anything about this Bart,* the voice lied. *Mr. La Fontaine and I have been friends for many years,* the voice finally continued after a considerable delay.

Why this contrivance? Rachel asked with growing irritation.

But tell me, the woman responded by way of reply and clearly determined to keep the conversation under control. *The message was really very poor. We need to get a new machine,* and there was a peal of laughter

from the male in the background. *What was it you said at the end of your message?*
What I said was what my husband told me to tell you. He said you should remember The Wall, and something about remember how weak it was, or they were, and her voice trailed away as she glanced up as John crept into the room dragging his blanket with him.
Just that. No specific Wall?
Just that, she said, taking the sleepy child into her arms. There was a muffled conversation which seemed to continue for an eternity as John started waking fretfully, and then the speaker returned with a greater clarity and keenness in her voice. *You have a child?* she asked immediately, though it was more statement than question. Then – without allowing the slightest pause for a reply- continued *If so, I suggest you and your child get the first transport out of London. I'll give you an address, and you can come here if you want. Bart, Mr. La Fontaine, would want that. Just you and your child- this is a close family thing. You understand? And as quickly as you can. No questions, just come today. If you don't, your child may be dead very soon.* Before Rachel could ask any further questions, she was given –very clearly, but only once -an address in the Sheffield SafeLands. Only once, and again the repetition that she must take the first available transport in the morning. Then the line went dead.

Las Palmas

05.17 UTC April 2nd

God had been so good to Captain John Matthew Adams that he found himself singing his favourite hymn as his landing craft chugged away from the shore. He had waited until last, ensured all was in place and then slipped away silently with his personal escort from their masterpiece near the peak, gliding almost silently down the gullies until they reached the beach. He had sensed, rather than seen, the arrival of the Europeans as his men had melted away, and a muffled explosion carrying over the waves was a poignant reminder of the complex of devices he had left to deter any enemy interference with his plan.

A glance at his watch reminded him of how dramatically they had fallen behind the original schedule. As always, he assumed that such changes were all part of The Lord God's divine plan. He had been reassured by direct contact with President Smith who refined their plans in the light of the Storm. However, even allowing for this, there had been some additional slippage. The European had apparently been re-enforced both in terms of numbers and the arrival of some heavier weapons. Despite pressure from his own men, he had refused the use of his own heavier guns. They had been transported to suppress any opposition earlier in their mission, but his own calculations allowed little scope for their use on this slope. Fearful of the consequences of European fire, he had urged greater speed on his command. The result had been a steady trickle of martyrs joining The Lord.

The slippage in time was not in itself highly significant, although Adams knew that Smith had planned for a symbolically important combination of times and days; but at least the installation had been successfully completed. However, a quick calculation of the distance between their current position and the African coast did give him cause for concern. Given the new timing agreed with President Smith, there was considerable pressure to make landfall and move inland. Not an impossible task, but one which would require God's Grace in granting them favourable winds and weather, and for now the wind was still driving high waves down from the north. True, once they had rounded the most northerly tip and passed Isla Graciosa their route would be almost due east, but there was no certainty that the weather would aid them.

Safely aboard the Omega, Adams went straight to the bridge, the water pouring from him leaving a clear trail. The ship's captain was busy there, the engines already vibrating and the distinct clatter of the anchor demonstrating the urgency of their departure. *A private word Christian Brother Chambers,* Adams panted, still recovering from his sprint up to the bridge. *New orders.*

As you wish Brother Sir. And your orders?

We are sailing south. To this place, and he stabbed a finger on the chart in front of them. *This Tarfaya area is closer, and the Lord has informed me that we shall not reach the safety of our first destination in time.*

And the rest of the squadron Brother, Sir?

We shall join with them, Adams lied instantly. He had already decided they were doomed. *It will add what, about 150 miles to our journey? But we can reach them by this road* – and again a finger stabbed on the map- *within a few days at most.*

You think so, Sir? Chambers enquired gently. He had been captain of the *Purity* until Adams had taken it into his head that a ship with such a name was the essential flagship for **his** mission. Not that Chambers felt aggrieved at essentially being deprived of his command without prior notice, but he did feel a sense of grievance that he was not privy to whatever Adams had been doing on the island, what was happening next, and why there was such a sudden urgency to reach the African mainland. Not that he would challenge orders – that was far too dangerous- but he did care about his ship and

his crew. *I wonder what kind of condition those roads are in?* he enquired tentatively. *And you really think it is wise to split our forces like this and…*
Our Lord has spoken to me, Adams retorted. *Do you wish to question this …?*
Certainly not Christian Brother, Sir. Impetuously, Chambers did not even permit Adams to finish the sentence. He had seen this line repeated time and time again by Smith, Monroe and now this young up-start, and on each occasion it had posed a threat to the life of those involved. This was not a fight he could win and, therefore, he would not pursue it. I was simply talking aloud Christian Brother, Sir he added hastily. *Worthless thoughts. The Lord is with us and will doubtless protect the path of the righteous…*and, realising that he had slipped unconsciously into Smith's favourite mantra, he cut himself short. *And with your permission, I'll set the new course and inform the squadron, Sir. With the wind and seas behind us, and the islands for protection, we shall, with God's blessing, make good speed.*

Las Palmas

05.18 UTC April 2nd

Anna Maria stood in the waves of drizzle which the wind was swishing in from the north across the ocean. She stared numbly at the pile of concrete in front of her. She had lost half a dozen good soldiers to booby traps reaching the site, with another ten injured, and now she was impotent. Everything the Christian Americans had left behind had been deliberately wrecked so that no tool or equipment could be used. It was indicative of the urgency with which this situation was being treated that a powered aircraft was even now braving the storm to try and parachute engineers and drilling equipment onto the site. All being well in their jump, they would try to undo whatever the '*American maniacs*' had been doing.

She had finally been fully briefed by Central Command in Madrid, and had realised with horror the implications of her failure to obey orders. She knew that she could face a court martial later, but in her heart she questioned if she and her small command could have done things differently. It was all very well for generals enjoying the warmth and security of command centres hundreds of kilometres removed to issue orders, but as the commander on the ground she had done what she could with the men and equipment at her disposition. To the surprise of the corporal standing by her side, she giggled loudly as the irrelevance of the potential court martial hit her. If what she had been told were true, she would be happy enough to survive the next day or two.

Twenty minutes later a puzzled squad from her command were jogging their way down the slopes of the mountain under strict orders to establish a base at the far, southern tip of the island. Drawn from different parts of old Spain and Portugal, and of different genders and ranks, they shared three things. Unknown to its members, all had been selected by Anna Maria as redundant to the current mission. All were under the age of thirty or, if over thirty had children and each had been selected in order to offer him, or her, a slim chance of survival.

Las Palmas

21.43 UTC April 2nd

How much time do we have? demanded the captain commanding the engineers. Ulf Hansen's team had landed with the paratroopers an hour earlier in a reckless act born of desperation. Landing in rough terrain in the dark and high wind, two men had been carried to their death over the edge and several seriously injured. Of much greater importance was the loss of three drill units to the sea. *No know,* Anna Maria replied, looking up and trying to fight the waves of fatigue which had brought her to the frontiers of sleep and destroyed her English. *A day? A hour? A minuto? Your intelligence not know?*

I know nothing, the captain replied, wiping another stream of mud-filled rain from his face. *I just had orders to land, dig out whatever they had buried, and then give what they had left behind to them.* He gesticulated to an ordnance team sitting under a tarpaulin draped skilfully between the shells of two Christian half-tracks which had been burnt out before they left. The man's impeccable English betrayed the slightest American accent from five years when his father had worked in Boston before the troubles had reached there, and the family had returned to Stuttgart. Over thirty years later, his face betrayed the concern and growing fear of someone ordered to sit on a powder keg with no knowledge of when it had been timed to explode.

So how many horas you need to drill? Anna Maria demanded. *They will be at land soon, and I think that will be the time.*

Then we have a problem, Hansen replied. *With only two drills, we can start planning for tomorrow's evening meal if we have to drill through this quality of concrete to the same depth for each shaft. You have any suggestions for our evening meal? Any local specialities?* He laughed nervously and mentally ticked a reassuring box entitled '*Wife and children safe with mother-in -law in Vienna.*'

Chapter VII
At The Pillars
The Straits of Gibraltar
06.19 UTC April 3th

The eastern horizon was slowly brightening in what promised to be the first clear sky for days. Monroe's anxiety was mounting in tune with the rising sun. They had made good speed through the night, and improvements in the weather and sea conditions had made it easier to deploy his main warships forward whilst slipping *Genesis* behind the forward screen of warships to both shepherd the straggling armada and protect his flagship.

Then, once again Smith had countermanded Monroe's orders. Rather than pushing through the Straits as rapidly as possible taking advantage of the cover of darkness, he had decided to hold what was what was essentially a revue so that he, Smith, could again be saluted and admired as the armada sailed past. Monroe could barely control his fury, remembering the chaos and delays this behaviour had caused earlier. Now, having received an encrypted confirmation from Adams that he had finished his work on Las Palmas, they were working desperately against the clock.

Thus far, Smith's vanity had resulted in a mere fifty vessels entering the western end of The Straits.

Barely an hour earlier, the armada's lead destroyer had encountered and sunk a small European coastguard cutter. Despite the jamming blanket generated by his counter- intelligence people, the vessel had managed to send a warning message prior to its destruction. This was now an irrelevance. Whether by coincidence, or a result of this prior-warning, the lead warships had encountered such stiff resistance towards the eastern end of The Straits that both the heavy destroyers *Leviticus* and *Abraham* had been destroyed. As always when faced with a slight set back, Smith had entered into yet another frenzy of self-recrimination and supplication to The Lord.

The European defences at Gibraltar had now been partially silenced, but they were so deeply entrenched in their fortifications overlooking The Straits that Monroe had been obliged to order several of his most heavily armoured vessels to destroy the remaining shore installations whilst his main body attempted to slip past in the southern channel.

This was not supposed to be happening. Since the time of the Middle Eastern and Afghan wars decades earlier, the common opinion amongst both Federal and Christian Confederal Americans was that the Europeans feared battle and would abandon their positions under fire. *'Had this not been the case at Las Palmas?'* Monroe asked himself. *Or had Adams lied?* Here though, the Europeans were putting up a stiff resistance, and his only consolation was that there had been no fire from the southern shore. Intelligence was unsure as to whether European or Arab forces occupied the northern African shores, but Monroe suspected the latter. However, no sooner had he concluded that '*Praise be to God! The Arabs are either too disorganised or fearful to interfere,'* than he rued the thought. Recognising the hated Christian-American ensign, a Caliphate battery stationed near Tangier launched its missiles. Old and slow, they were intercepted relatively easily, but as a precaution Monroe had ordered yet more warships forward. The result was to create only a narrow channel through which his transports could filter.

Theoretically he had the air and fire power to totally eliminate what were effectively independent and mutually-hostile enemies. In reality, though he would admit it to no one, even God appeared to be conspiring with Smith to frustrate his best endeavours. He faced the classic dilemma of a commander whose power could not be brought to bear because of the limited common front with the enemy. This was compounded by the double conundrum of a commander whose airpower had been rendered useless. During the night the wind had shifted from the north to a more westerly direction. This had speeded their journey, but the strong westerly was driving the Atlantic's waters into the narrow channel of The Straits and creating mountainous waves. The sophisticated gun and missile systems of his warships were unaffected, but it left him unable to launch his remaining aircraft or to effectively use the relatively primitive weapons which had often simply been welded onto the docks of the previously civilian vessels which constituted the vast majority of his fleet. Consequently, Monroe suddenly found himself dramatically reduced in military capability when he needed it.

Nuova Lisboa

06.19 UTC April 3rd

Henry had been sitting in the mess hall eating breakfast with Marie-Claire and her crew when battle stations sounded. They had all been woken early with the promise of better weather and a dawn flight down to the Cadiz-Jerez airbase and military station. They had been informed that the high command was now working on the basis of Henry's theory and was marshalling its forces on the assumption that the Christian-American fleet would either attempt to force an entry into the

Mediterranean or seize land along the coastal belt in preparation for such an eventuality. Henry had no great confidence in the accuracy of his own analysis; it was simply an educated calculation based on the limited evidence to hand and Smith's eccentricities. If he were correct, there was no saying when events would unfold, though the certainty had to be that it would be after Smith's ships had reached safety.

The base was already buzzing with rumours that several large transports had braved the storms to fly down to Las Palmas. According to some, they were carrying nearly two hundred paratroopers and a missile battery or –less credibly it was said- sophisticated drilling rigs. Marie-Claire had come off duty around midnight and, joining, Henry in his quarters, had confided that drilling rigs rather than missiles had indeed been stowed aboard the aircraft along with a team of military engineers and several platoons of paratroopers.

Her own guess was that they were going to try and undo the work of Smith's forces, though whether the Europeans had sent enough troops to dislodge them was unknown. These, she assured him, were all the aviation fuel transports available in the south western command area,

though additional aircraft were flying in from other commands. These were loaded with more troops.

The dirigibles were being readied for flight as soon as weather conditions permitted which, Marie-Claire believed, would be that morning.
Do you want to come south with us, she had suddenly demanded *or is it time to go back to your family? If you believe your work ere is finished?*
He looked at her with both surprise and …and something else. There was too much sentiment in her voice for it to be a purely technical question. Whilst Henry had kept telling himself that the emotions he felt for her were either based purely on physical attraction, or the stresses arising from the current crisis, in moments of honesty he knew there was something more. Perhaps it was something so banal as an attraction arising from the uniform, and he remembered his mother joking about what she had described as the *pulling power of a pilot's uniform*, but there was something about this woman which made Rachel appear thin and insipid. Perhaps he had never been fully happy with her, but now they had a son to support and .... well, he was weak enough to have affairs, but not hard enough to break her heart.
Do I actually have a choice? he'd asked, the tenor and surprise in his voice unintentionally revealing his own emotions. The decision had been made for him before breakfast when he returned to his room

to change. A note containing an order from the base commander to travel south with the morning flights had been slipped under his door. He had no idea as to whether Amanda had received the same notification, or indeed if she had organised it. Not that there was any precise indication as to whom he was to fly with. Henry's initial assumption was that they knew he was sleeping with one of their officers, considered this to be a negligible security risk, and believed that he might be of some use at some uncertain point in the future. When he had thought about it further, he concluded that the Europeans probably considered it wiser to keep him and any knowledge he might have gleaned away from London, and by extension away from Washington. Doubtless, European intelligence might still be considering the possibility that his theories were intended as a diversion in part of a larger game, and his passion towards Marie-Claire suddenly chilled as he remember her earlier threat. *What was it she had said? That she would willingly put a bullet in his brain?*

So breakfast found Henry awash both with unusually good RealCoffee and conflicting sentiments. The sirens found him abandoned as the air crews hurried to the briefing area, though their silencing coincided with Amanda's appearance. He could not prevent himself enquiring with whom she

had spent the night with this time. The reaction he provoked was a wry smile, a slight parting of her lips and a small serpentine flick of her tongue. You could have had some too she pouted before she poured an enormous glass of black coffee. '*Drank too much again last night,'* Henry mused and was about to say something to that effect when Marie-Claire dashed back into the mess, a spare flight suit in her arms. *Come,* she *demanded get into this. When you are ready in cinque minutes I have permission for you to come with me and see what the Americans are doing. Perhaps you can help us again with their next plan.*
And me? Amanda demanded, clearly peeved that her seniority was being infringed.
You are to stay here and communicate with your government, Marie-Claire replied crisply. *That is the order I have received. You are to go to the central communications after your breakfast. They wait for you there so you can speak with your government when we speak to you – you will be, a .... a relay person I think you say.*
But, why are you taking him? He can talk to you from here. Amanda demanded, her honour less than satisfied and resentment growing that Marie-Claire would enjoy Henry rather than herself.
Sometimes seeing is useful, and he may be able to see some of what the Americans do. If you want to argue you must talk so someone more important... I am obeying orders. Come,

quickly! she demanded again, turning to Henry. She strode off, him hopping behind whilst trying to get a second leg into his suit. As the pair finally exited through the mess doors, Amanda was almost certain that she heard her say something about ... *no room for fucking on the dirigibles..* but the doors swung shut before the alcohol enabled her to think of a coherent reply.

Outside, the significance of developments was evident as the runways were suddenly full of motorized units buzzing about and carrying crews to more remote parts of the base. Slower units crawled across the tarmac towing aircraft, the slowest munitions. Within minutes, a transport had taken them to Marie-Claire's craft, one of the latest generation replacing her older one which had ultimately proven irreparable.

Two fighter bombers were cradled beneath its straining lanyards, and Henry's quick head-count suggested a crew of at least six including the pilots and gunners but with no evident aircraft crews. It crossed his mind for the first time that perhaps the dirigible crews were dual role, with the dirigible pilots later flying the aircraft, but he left the question unspoken.

Looking up, he noted that at least thirty other craft were already airborne and drifting rapidly southwards. A quick check of some broken clouds revealed that they were being carried by fresh winds, but the urgency of the situation was again made apparent when the first engines spluttered into life. The old propeller systems would add a good two hundred knots with a following wind, but the Europeans would not be burning through the fuel unless they were deeply concerned about something.

His calculations were interrupted when a powerfully-built ground-crew thrust a parachute and life-support system into his hands and something else which he recognised, after some delay, as some kind of body armour. Then, a heavy helmet was pushed firmly and unceremoniously onto his head and he immediately found himself propelled up a ladder, through an open hatch, and into the fuel scented interior of the dirigible itself. He had already been warned several times by different aircrews that this was not the time to delay, for within minutes the craft would be rising into the air. If his helmet and life-support were not properly connected, he could soon find himself either freezing in the morning cold or gasping for breath as they rose to a higher altitude. His struggle with the various, unfathomable hoses became more desperate as the hatch was hauled shut and he felt the cables which had been holding them to the ground blocks released.

Sit down. I help, suddenly boomed in his helmet intercom. Looking us from the quandary as to which tubes carried hot air from the engines and which oxygen, he found a small figure standing over him. The uniform epaulets indicated that this was one of the gunners who served as desperate line of defence if the cumbersome crafts were stripped of their fighter cover. Like most dirigible crew, this one was short and slightly built and, looking through her primary visor he was shocked at the apparent youth. *'Could she be more than sixteen?'* he found himself thinking, though as if to prove that youth was no handicap he suddenly found himself slammed deep into his chair and the tubes deftly connected. *Put your belt on Sir, and your sun visor she needs to be down soon,* boomed the voice, and as if to end any further speculation about her age she deftly pulled down her own mirrored visor. Dragging her tubes behind her, she shambled back to the starboard gun port.

Peering out through a porthole on his side of the dirigible, and with the limited view this offered, he quickly appraised the line of dirigibles gyrating around Marie-Claire's craft. Launching had appeared a rather ad hoc, hurried affair, though he was none the wiser as to the exact cause for the haste. Now they were under way and moving southwards at an increasing speed, the dirigibles were clearly forming up in what was going to be their battle formation. Even to his amateurish eyes, it was clear that the symbols within the European flag either indicated different countries or squadrons or both.

Fighting the nausea arising from the speed of their ascent and the pockets of turbulence they were already encountering, Henry glanced at his watch, and then at the sun's rays which streamed through the starboard portholes as both they and the sun climbed in the sky. '*Nuova Lisboa was what, some two hundred miles from the Straits of Gibraltar?*' he asked himself. '*If we fly at full speed we will be in the area well within an hour even in the dirigibles… but what was it Marie-Claire had said? That the fighters were always released at what she had called 'Point O'.*' Apparently there was a point at which the fighters could be released and had time to form-up at their battle height with the maximum conservation of aviation fuel. *It was,* she had explained carefully, *the best way to maintain both combat capability and give the fighters the possibility of finding an airfield to land. A way of minimising losses of both crews and machines.*

Suddenly, he realised that he could just make out the foremost dirigibles as vague blobs against the lightening blue -dawn sky. They had swung further east, and a scene from an ancient film came into his mind. *'What had it been called again? Something like 'Toro! Toro!? Tora! Tora!?'? Or was that the old Spanish word for a bull? They are going to attack from the morning sun,* he confirmed to himself, though in the back of his mind he questioned how effective this technique would be against modern electronic systems.

Then Marie-Claire's co-pilot's voice boomed in his helmet, in the stilted, semi-English which the majority of officers used. This time is was clearly overlaid with a strong Spanish accent. *Battle amber. Enemy contact estimated thirty minutes.* he enounced carefully, and Henry noticed both gunners re-checking their weapons.

The Straits of Gibraltar
06.42 UTC April 3rd

Monroe's heavily armed vanguard had managed to largely silence the guns and missile batteries on the Gibraltar side and the Caliphate's fire had ceased. His armada was now sailing through at maximum speed using both its engines and the following wind in their sails. The passage had not been without losses. In addition to the two warships lost in the first exchanges, he had lost *The Gethsemane,* another capital ship; another three had been seriously damaged and three transports and two Soul carriers sunk. Other ships reported varying degree of damage, but on balance his losses had been relatively light so far.

The reality was that only a small part of the fleet had completed the passage, and with every passing minute he feared the risk of European re-enforcements arriving. The other captains must have shared his concerns, for a collective tension was spreading across the armada, and Monroe had struggled to prevent a free-for-all which risked vessels colliding as they jockeyed for position in the narrow channel. A further, serious complication arose from the seriously damaged vessels which wallowed as smoldering hulks and further impeded passage. After a heated discussion with Smith, Monroe was ordered to turn the fleet's own guns on them. This was again a difficult decision. Immediately before he had ordered the vessels sunk, survivors had been reported scaling down netting into the sea, and desperate call for assistance received from below deck. Smith again avoided direct association with the deed, and simply observed it was a matter of saving as many lives as possible.

Over forty ships were now either on the

Mediterranean side, or in the Straits itself, as though in accordance with some master plan. Smith would claim this was the case, though inwardly he would be furious at the slight on his status arising from any losses. Monroe licked his lips nervously at the prospect of Tuckman and his cronies finding a way to blame himself. However, with luck he would be able to argue that *'God's elite'* had been chosen to make the final journey to New Jerusalem and that the other Souls had been chosen to meet their maker more immediately as part of God's master plan. *'God moves in mysterious ways,'* was such a useful part of Smith's armoury and he might well accept the idea.

Monroe glanced again anxiously at his watch. Time was now critical. He had, reluctantly, resigned himself to the potential loss of some stragglers, but the horrendous prospect now loomed that there was perhaps insufficient time to ensure the passage of a large part of the convoy. There was nothing he could do now– Adams was the deciding factor. He had earlier ordered the engines on *Genesis* to be cut back in order to allow other warships to lead the vanguard and silence the opposition he had anticipated in The Straits. Though an immensely large and powerful vessel, the very size of his flagship made it an obvious target in the narrow channel and he failed to share Smith's resignation at the prospect of immediate martyrdom. That could be left to braver, more dedicated Souls, or those who simply obeyed his orders.

For now, he realised with growing concern that he and *Genesis* risked being left stranded on the Atlantic side of the Straits and he ordered full speed to be made, cutting across the bows of a large Soul carrier in his haste. Almost simultaneously the reports came in that the vanguard of his forces were coming under fire from missile batteries stationed to the east in the mountains at Renda. Monroe bit his lips in frustration, drawing a slight trickle of blood which ran slowly down his chin. Again, his thoughts turned to the intelligence reports which had convinced him that the Europeans remained a spent force after the last conflicts, and that he was would face minimal resistance. Given the scale of the opposition around Gibraltar, he had hoped that this reflected the extent of the European capability. Now, looking at the charts, he was forced to face the unpalatable possibility that he might face effective, organised opposition for fifty miles or more along the old Spanish coast.

Chapter VIII
Crusaders
Tarfaya, Old Kingdom of Morocco.
Western Caliphate.
06.20 UTC April 3rd

Two parallel strips fronting the Atlantic Ocean constituted Tarfaya. The old town sat with its feet in the Atlantic Ocean, the highest tides lapping several inches into the cafes, shops and the odd residence which had once proudly over-looked the sea. The Storms churned water through the same buildings, each episode eroding more of the mud brick or concrete walls, or increasingly collapsing an entire edifice. Towards the remains of the port, a rusting oil rig stood on the beach where it had been driven by the Storms. It listed precariously out to sea, gaping holes and missing struts witness to the value of the scrap metal which had been scavenged. The remaining metal was testimony to the inability to remove more without additional loss of life

Some two hundred yards inland, a second row of buildings survived despite the sea. The ten thousand or so inhabitants eked out a living in a bad year through fishing, bartering the smoked or salted catch to towns further inland in exchange for vegetables and clothing. In a good year there was enough rain to grow sufficient vegetables for local consumption, and in such good times income from sales could be used to repair houses and transport, buy livestock, or even small domestic appliances. At the north end of the town the crumbling walls and neglected perimeter of an old military base were testimony to the region's neglect by what passed as the local government. It was still garrisoned by a dozen or so para-military police, but they rarely dared to venture out except to shop and collect their monthly rations and pay.

Tarfaya had once been a relatively prosperous city of over half a million, feeding off the oil exploration out in the Atlantic waters. The airstrip abutting the base had bustled with the arrival and departure of light aircraft, and there had even been some limited tourism in the form of adventurous Europeans. Then, the oil fields had been abandoned with the growth of Atlantic Storms. True, the developed, capped fields had continued producing for some years, buried relatively safely beneath the surface. However, further development had been halted as the Storms had eventually overwhelmed even the most robust and sophisticated drilling rigs and eventually servicing even the existing wells had started to prove too risky or expensive. Now, the weeds poking through the runway were disturbed only by grazing goats and camels, and this had been the case for almost a decade.

As almost everywhere, declining living standards and the return of real or comparative poverty had been a boon for religion. Tarfaya's main mosque was evidence of this, being almost unique in remaining structurally sound, flourishing in its use and increasing in power and influence. Despite this, poverty resulted in decay and the inevitable failure of the electrics. So it was that this morning Hama Al-Hamsa, the mosque's elderly muezzin, was obliged to climb the minaret's worn stairs to call the faithful to prayer with the power of his voice alone.

It was not yet quite dawn, but he knew that he would need time to recover from his exertions before his lungs would enable him to start the call to Fajr. Once, the loud speakers topping the minaret had obviated any need for exertion on his part, but the electricity had failed some twenty years ago. Pausing at the top of the stairs to catch his breath, he shuffled out onto the balcony to view the ocean at leisure for the first time in days. Until now, he had hurried best he could, done his duty, and then fled down in the face of the wind and rain. For a moment his thoughts turned to his childhood back in Oman- a happier life in happier time. As he did so, something out at sea caught his attention.

Carefully putting on his glasses, he stared in surprise at the cluster of boats sailing directly towards the harbour. It was their bows slicing through the waves which had attracted his attention – no local boat could do that. Then, an educated man, he started in disbelief as he recognised the Christian American flag with the zealots' crosses substituting the stars of the Federal flag. Seconds later Tarfaya woke early, not to the call to prayer, but the call to arms.

Thirty miles west of The Straits of Gibraltar
06.49 UTC April 3rd

Lagard had ordered battle stations onboard La Cité as soon as the first reports arrived of the developing battle in The Straits. Somebody, somewhere, in WashingtonWall or Montreal had convinced the Europeans to give him access to their communication codes, and so it was that he could access at least some of the growing buzz of military communications across southern Europe. It seemed that the Gibraltar garrison had initially inflicted some damage on the American fleet, with – it seemed- some incidental assistance from the Muslim forces to the southern coast. Now, there was an ominous silence from the European garrison.

That morning Lagard had been briefed of the reports that Monroe had recently used his tactical nuclear weapons against the Federal American military. He was now eager to close with the enemy on the assumption that close-proximity would reduce the likelihood of their using their nuclear capability on him. *Hopefully*, he reasoned with his officers *these people are still sane enough to avoid minimising their own casualties.* However, in the back of his mind was the doubt that there would be much difference in this between Christian and Muslim extremists.

Tactically, an additional motivator in closing with the Monroe's fleet was the strategic advantage of engaging a numerically superior enemy on a narrow front. It was a lesson which was drilled into every Canadian officer in training, using the example of Greeks against the Persians at Thermopylae and the recent- some would say the even more glorious- stand by Quebec's troops and volunteers against American forces at the battle of Fort William Henry.

Glancing at the chart in front of them, Lagard and his tactical warfare team had instantly agreed that the bottleneck of The Straits would provide minimal opportunity for the enemy to use their advantage in numbers. Moreover, they would almost certainly be focused on what lay ahead rather than behind. Messages from the Federal forces, transposed onto an Atlantic map, showed the first ships in the far distance and the blip of a solitary Federal submarine still several hours away. These forces would arrive long after the vast American armada had made its way into the Mediterranean, though Lagard was puzzled -had they created a trap of a safe haven for themselves? *Monroe's probably going to either mine the area or, if he knows that he is being pursued, he'll wait to use the Straits as a natural defensive position,* volunteered Singh.

Or they'll keep running, Mullard ventured. *The further they are into the Mediterranean the closer they are to this religious objective of theirs and I doubt we can believe Smith is such a fool as to arrive uninvited. That means he'll have access to fuel and reinforcements at some point, while we, and them-* he added jabbing his finger at the map *will be out of fuel and ...well, what is the current relationship between the Federals and the Europeans? Love or war?*

I'm not really interested, Lagard snapped, revealing the stresses of the past days. *This is an opportunity to take out some Yankee ships, and I'm not much concerned which part of their mess they are from.* The murmur of agreement around the table said much about the hatred of Americans following the Arctic Wars. *So,* he continued emphatically *advice on the best strategy for maximum damage -with minimum risk if you please.*

Five thousand metres above the northern Huelva marshes.

07.01 UTC April 3rd

Huelva water, was the reply Henry had finally obtained. He had gesticulated several times to the gunner in the seat diagonally in front, trying to identify the stretches of water with the odd island which seemed to sit endlessly beneath them. *More like Huelva bloody marshes,* Henry spat to himself, frustrated that his abuse of the intercom had resulted in his system being turned off. He had only tried to crack a couple of jokes to raise morale, but Marie-Claire had been furious at what she deemed his *blocking* of the system and had shut him down half way through the third joke. Not that he was really sure that his humour was appreciated, but a number of helmets had been turned constantly in his direction. Now, it was clear that there had been a change in plan, or they were waiting for something, because they had been moving forward at a snail's pace for some ten minutes.

Marie-Claire sat in the command seat of the dirigible listening to the stream of anti-British jokes passing between the crew. Henry's crude attempt at humour, typical unfathomable British humour was the general consensus, had touched raw nerves amongst some of the older crew with direct experience of confronting the British and their American allies. There was also a considerable under-current of resentment that he had been brought aboard at a time when the craft was about to enter combat, and when every additional gram could reduce their speed and agility.

Not that she was blamed to her face, there was too much personal respect and observance of her rank for that, but there must have been unspoken questions as to whether her judgement had been warped by what was considered a less than professional relationship with *the English one.* She was puzzled herself. The only reason she could think of that she had been ordered to bring him on the mission was to keep him away from the English bitch – a much more dangerous piece of work it was accepted. Though how either of them could be of either value or danger now was beyond her. All the evidence seemed to confirm Henry's original wild guess had been accurate, though precisely what the Christian crazies were planning was still a matter of conjecture. For now, her irritation and growing tension was focused on ensuring that the American ships were either destroyed or turned back.

Looking at the deck electronics, she felt a slight tremor of pride, mixed with surprise, at the nature of the military forces her tactical warfare systems could see taking position across the horizon. To the east, a battle squadron was sailing out from Marseille while further east still another squadron was starting to appear on her screen as it sailed at full speed from the new base at Genoa. In all, she had been informed that no fewer than forty eight warships – nearly the entire Mediterranean fleet – were taking up position to block the American advance. Given the pathetic state of Europe's defences after the last clashes, huge amount of money must have been expended on these new vessels and the weapons profile on her data base suggested the Americans would not have such an easy time on this occasion.

Of immediate interest to her flight were two squadrons of fighter bombers coming in from France under their own power. She had been informed that they were of the latest *Rasoir* class and could match any aircraft the Americans were known to possess, but it concerned Marie-Claire that their fuel reserves would already be depleted by the time they arrived. *'Just how much combat time will they have?'* she demanded of herself. The haste of their arrival might prove to be a problem, but the

immediate reasoning was clear. For now, the need was to engage with the enemy before they could launch their air cover, but allowing for this she could not understand why they had been ordered to maintain the current holding pattern. *Surely we should attack now and not wait for these aircraft to join the main battle group!* she exclaimed to her co-pilot. He shrugged his shoulders and simply replied *Orders.*
The areas to the south and west were less clear, with the American electronic jamming creating a haze which nothing had been able to penetrate effectively. *Wisely*, in Marie-Claire's opinion, Central Command had ordered the release of several advanced drones which should now have finished their reconnaissance. Of some bemusement to her crew was a single orange dot moving rapidly from the west and closing on the tail of the American formation. They had been briefed that some poor fool of a captain from Free Canada had been ordered by his government to chase the Christians across the Atlantic, though what he hoped to achieve with just one vessel was a matter of much speculation. *He is certainly very fast and quite large*, Marie-Claire mused, momentarily focusing the sensors on that vessel. But her thoughts were disturbed as a voice in her helmet broke in to announce the results from the drone flights. She was

too slow to question the data as at least a dozen voices were quicker than her own. When the babble stopped, her face had already blanched -as had that of her co-pilot. He looked at her quizzically.

You understand what I understand ? he demanded, doubt evident in his voice.

What do you understand? she replied with a nervous laugh.

I understand environ 428 ship. About quatre cent vingt huit American ships. And you?

I understand we are going to have an ell of a bataille. I do not believe in a god, but if there is one I shall pray that I want these ships not to be all warships.

The Straits

07.04 UTC April 3rd

Twenty four year old second lieutenant William Tyke, half-monitoring the primary intelligence consoles on the *Genesis,* had already decided that he was not going to admit to having missed the drones fly past. At twenty four years of age, he had witnessed enough of the punishments that Smith – and Monroe when in a rarer, bad mood- could mete out to what were deemed negligent crew. His immediate, personal, plans were for a wife and family in New Eden - not at the rope end of what Smith liked to call his hanging parties. It wasn't his fault anyway, or so he was convinced. He had already been busy monitoring the European forces massing to their north and then aircraft had appeared on the scanners monitoring beyond the eastern horizon. Inevitably, a flood of confirmations and requests for orders had come in at the very minute that Smith had suddenly arrived on deck, demanded of Monroe how many ships had successfully entered the Mediterranean, and capriciously decided that seventy was a good enough number to justify a celebration.

He'd seen Monroe protesting, but Smith had insisted, and his crony Tuckman had suddenly appeared with a couple of bottles of champagne which had been opened and poured into tiny glasses. True, probably not enough alcohol to affect battle performance, but essential crew had been taken from their posts at a critical time. If anyone ever got round to reviewing stored data they might notice Tyke's omission, but it was a reassuring thought he was not technically answerable to that part of the air defence

He could see the consternation on Monroe's face. They had yet to get a single aircraft in the air and, while not personally privy to any timetable, it was clear from Monroe's agitated, constant glances at the main consoles, and the way that he was worrying his lips, that he was seriously concerned about time. Even to Tyke's relatively inexperienced eyes, it was apparent that there was some kind of deadline involved here. It briefly occurred to him that Smith might have arranged a rendezvous with the Judaic brethren, who everyone knew had a considerable military capability and no great love of the Europeans. He immediately dismissed this idea from his mind – in recent years they were not known to stray so far from religious homeland. Meanwhile, Smith appeared oblivious to Monroe's concerns – *Another of his religious experiences,* the lieutenant mumbled to himself in a temporary lapse. He was reassured when a quick glance confirmed that no one was within hearing distance.

Chapter IX
Clockwork
Ten years earlier

Chinese companies had been well established in the Nigerian economy for well over forty years, using the plentiful, cheap and sometimes skilled workforce as a near-market substitute for their own. Initially, cheap Nigerian oil had been the decider in decision-making, both companies and the national government seeing the flow of capital from sales as more significant than the employment loss from moving even more jobs out of China itself. The industrial belt along the coast, and around the one-time capital Lagos, were usually favoured because of their the proximity to the ports and the vital oil pipelines carrying the fuel without which China's factories would grind to a halt within hours. Labour costs were also low, Nigerian demographic growth having started to rise again as Islam became a more important religion. The area had thus offered the golden combination of low-waged, skilled workers with access to energy and relative proximity to the European markets.

So it was that an electronic component with the serial number ZR23D184 had been born late, one hot, stinking, summer Friday afternoon when the quality control team for Xintao Electronic

Corporation could think of little more than the prospects of a cold beer and the evening match between two local teams. The Head of Quality Control, an otherwise important step in the production process, was busy in the process of getting one of the employees pregnant behind a mountain of crates waiting to be shipped. And so – by one of those quirks of fates which so often decide human destiny- the Navy of the American Confederation was ultimately to acquire a consignment of timers which had escaped any inspection. Not that John Matthew Adams and his team from the Christian Confederation Navy could ever have suspected this. Prior to shipment on one of the last regular Atlantic convoys, the timers had acquired cartons attesting to their quality, precision and strict adherence to US Military norms. It was the best packaging that Chinese and Nigerian industrial piracy could provide.

One mile offshore.
Tarfaya, Old Kingdom of Morocco.
Western Caliphate.
07.18 UTC April 3rd

Despite the morning cool, Adams was sweating profusely on *Omega's* bridge. Initially, he had attributed it to the early stages of a fever, but had reluctantly recognised it as a reflection of the tension and fear that a true soldier of The Lord should not experience. However, things were not quite going to plan, and even a soldier of The Lord had the right to feel some anxiety for his future and family. It was not that The Lord condoned suicide, indeed that was an abhorrence which was only mitigated if the sacrifice resulted in the destruction of infidels, but Adams was aware that death would soon be the inevitable outcome if they failed to act with greater haste.

Being detected was an unexpected factor. He had assumed the village -or was it still a town?- would be asleep and if there were some kind of defence it would not be wasting its time looking out to sea. It was probably too far north for Nigerian raiders? The mosque had escaped his calculation, an elementary mistake for a man who declared himself so steeped in religious study. The rough sea and inexperienced gunners had ensured that the wailing from the minaret took some time to silence, though that was largely symbolic for the entire place would have been woken by the first shell. But Adams felt a degree of vindictiveness towards whoever was wailing from the top of the minaret, and honour would have been more easily satisfied if the warning cries had been terminated within the first dozen shells.

Now, machine gun and some semi-automatic shots, complemented by fire from a single artillery piece, were coming from a number of building fronting onto the beach and what appeared to be some kind of decayed military installation to his north. His plan here had always been simplicity itself – steer the ships at full speed as far as possible up the sand and shingle beach, drop the transports' bow noses, and then drive straight off. Then it was through the settlement and out onto the old national road leading south. It wasn't the direction he ultimately intended to travel, but it took his men away from the coast and gave them some height and protection. There was no return of fire from his side. His troops were already clambering into the amphibious half-tracks on the deck whilst the ship's crew were removing the last of the restraints holding them in position.

With only a matter of a few hundred yards to the beach, he ordered the autopilot engaged and the bridge abandoned before hurrying down onto the deck and clambering into the lead vehicle. Almost immediately there was a grating sound as the *Omega*'s flattened keel gouged its way over some small rocks, and then the ships slewed onto the beach. There was a few second's delay during which, even with the futile roar from the still-revving engines, bullets could be heard splattering against the armoured front ramp. Then, on his order, the bow sections on all the vessels crashed down simultaneously and the first of *Omega's* vehicles lurched forward, speeding down the ramp and onto the beach. Instantly, it ground to an abrupt halt as an amphibian from the *Purity,* which had beached to their left, cut across its path.

Both vehicles stalled momentarily, time enough for three of the men in his vehicle to fall mortally injured before his own heavy machine guns and those on the other vehicles could suppress the enemy's fire. Then they were all moving, spitting sand and pebbles behind them until they hit the dirt track leading to the old N1. The lead vehicle maintained an almost incessant stream of fire, trying to ensure that none of the locals could effectively target them, and then they were clear of buildings and speeding south on the battered remnants of the main road. *Shit, we are running very late,* Adams cursed openly when he glanced at his watch, and a silent stream of profanities, mixed with devout prayers, followed.

LondonWall

07. 23 UTC April 3rd

Rachel La Fontaine had slept badly. John had woken several times early in the night, before her friend's antibiotics had started to fully work and reduce his pain. He had slept well from around three, but Rachael's mind continued to whirl, confused with the revelations of the last few days. John was still sleeping peacefully, but Rachael sat half-awake on her favourite place on the sofa carefully scrutinising the travel credits in her hand.

Theoretically, Henry's rank allowed them a total of a thousand miles of land travel a year, though that was definitely a theory. Actually getting a place on either a train or coach was difficult without a *priority card* from the government or one of the large companies, and the reliability of both means of transport was such that most people avoided long distance travel unless they had no choice. And she had a choice? Henry had been adamant that she leave and go, for whatever mysterious reason, to this sister who had suddenly appeared from the void. But Henry was less than reasonable at times, didn't have a sick child to care for, and had given her no tangible reason to leave the support of her friends and the comfort and safety of his – she corrected herself to 'their' – flat. No, she was not going to move. London was one of the safest places in England, had one of the best Walls and she was not going to take her son on a mad journey to meet a relative who had suddenly materialised – doubtless a creation of one of Henry's drunken or more eccentric spells. She looked once again at her watch, and decided to go back to bed.

Five thousand metres above the Huelva marshes.

07.36 UTC April 3rd

The sensors on Marie-Claire's dirigible were awash with data. To the east, several squadrons of allied aircraft were forming up in attack waves. The fighters, clearly evident by their smaller image and greater speed, were now in position as a shield immediately in front of the slower fighter bombers. Though she was not privy to the grand strategy, it seemed to her that was there was a simple plan to overwhelm the American air defences in a simultaneous two-pronged attack from both the north east and north west. She had her own reservations about splitting forces in this manner, but it also meant that the Americans would be forced to fight on two fronts. While a few surface craft were closing on the Americans, her guess was they were to act as a minor irritant and possibly stall the Christian advance until the main fleet arrived – the current presence was a match for nothing except lightly armed transports. So far they had not launched any air cover of their own, and even from Marie-Claire's altitude enough turbulence was visible on the Atlantic to explain why. T*hey would have to be mad or desperate to try and launch in that*, she murmured to her co-pilot pointing out to sea.

Yes, but it will be different once they are through the Straights, he almost snapped. *What are we waiting for Captain? We are wasting our fuel holding place with this wind behind us. We should be attacking while we have the advantage and...* The sentence remained unfinished as the very order he had been demanding came through on their helmets. Carefully checking the air space around her, Marie-Claire ordered her squadron to move forward at full speed and the pilots to start boarding their aircraft. A tap on her shoulder and a pointed finger brought her back to the main console. The Americans were launching aircraft from a carrier which had entered the Mediterranean, and Red dots were now swarming onto her console.

Houston: Four Years Earlier

John Matthew Adams was having another bad night. He had been to church twice that Sunday and during the afternoon had been honoured to hear newly re-elected President Smith talk of the need to cleanse God's Elect of the impurities of the liberal, heathen WUCCIES. It had been a rousing speech, though by its end Adams had concluded that much needed to be done to actually achieve Smith's goal of a 'New Jerusalem' or 'New Eden'. What was it? Even President Smith –God Bless Him- tended to change the name from time to time. Finally, he had flopped out of bed, crept through the Junior Officer's Dorm, and made himself a cup of something which claimed to be coffee. The room claimed to be the off-duty mess, but it could accommodate fewer than a dozen of the fifty, less one, men now sleeping in the dorm.

The previous year Adams had graduated with a degree in geography and mineralogy from one of the better North Carolinian universities. His family had applied enormous pressure on him to finish the degree, though he had increasingly questioned its value. On graduating, he had immediately decided to join the Christian Confederation Navy in order to serve the cause. Smith's speech had left him with an immediate, burning, desire to do something more and now- hence his insomnia. Sitting in the dim light of the mess room, he flicked through the old magazine which had been lying on his bedside table. The *National Geographic* was well over ten years old, one of the last to be published, its corners frayed and the paper rapidly yellowing. He had been carrying the magazine around with him for months waiting for the opportunity to read it, but he was determined to read a couple of articles listed on the front page which had caught his attention . He finished the first, made himself a second cup of disgusting CoffeeSimulant, in clear breach of regulations, and was about to start the second article when he dropped the magazine. It fell open at a page on The Canaries. He glanced briefly at the title and was about to turn the page when he stopped, turned back, and re-read the headline. *Yes!* he had shouted into his cup. *Brilliant!*

It had taken him two months of persistent badgering before he had been able to talk directly to one of Smith's staff who had then put him contact with Tuckman. Within the same week he was talking directly to God's Prophet himself. The following week he had been given power to select his own team to work on the project, to identify and requisition the ships, equipment and munitions he needed, and the valuable computer time to model the simulations he required. Nominally, he remained a lieutenant, but his rations and pay were increased to those of a full commander. Those who needed to know were made aware of his power and closeness to the President though Admiral Monroe remained in ignorance- in Adams's opinion an indication of the President's fundamental distrust.

Three weeks before their departure from RougeWall plans had been completed, and on Las

Palmas they had been implemented. President Smith had deemed it fit that the plan's execution should roughly coincide with sunrise-'A new dawn for the New Dawn.'- he had declared, though he had finally agreed to a rounded time, April 3rd 06.33 as a number that history would remember as the final riposte to the anti-Christs who had attempted to steal the Lord's kingdom. The 33 was, obviously, the human age of Jesus when crucified. Smith and he had debated an alternative deadline once it became clear that The Lord had signified his desire for an alternative deadline in the storm. As always, God had spoken to President Smith and informed him of the appropriateness of another time- April 3rd at 08.33.

The Straits of Gibraltar

07.43 UTC April 3rd

Rapidly approaching the western end of The Straits, La Cité's missiles were within range of the rear of Monroe's fleet. Lagard had ordered his weapons crews to await his instructions, reasoning that the Americans would be so occupied with the massing European - his sensors showed several squadrons of European dirigibles to the north east-that with luck they would regard his own arrival as that of one of their own stragglers.

Assuming that the Europeans had not suddenly accessed vast energy reserves, La Cité's tactical warfare team had initially assumed that they would follow the now classic military model in which each balloon would carry aircraft into the proximity of the battle zone before releasing them for combat. What puzzled him was why no aircraft were being launched, his perplexity turning to frustrated anger as the first Christian aircraft launched- Monroe had clearly managed to find calm water, which implied that his first carrier had entered the Mediterranean. Lagard suspected that whatever had caused the Europeans to delay would now cost them dearly in the fight to come. Of immediate concern was the realisation that the heavy seas he was still experiencing had caused him to neglect the possibility of an aircraft attack. These launches, although still limited to a bare dozen aircraft, changed the equation totally –despite the quality of its systems, La Cité could not fight and survive a simultaneous naval and air war against such odds.
Another concern–one that he hoped he was not communicating to his crew- was La Cité's relationship with the Europeans. Though his government had assured him that they had been notified of his presence and benign intentions, he had received no reply to his messages. Even the

briefest of replies would have been welcomed, for he was acutely aware that his ship could easily be mistaken as one of Smith's. Now, with the Christian air launch, the only chance for La Cité to survive would be to hope that his fire was attributed to the Europeans. Perhaps he could withdraw rapidly back into the Atlantic before Monroe's forces could locate the true source of the attack? It was, he admitted to himself, a fairly pathetic strategy. He now lacked the fuel to make the journey home, and the best outcome would be a rather ignominious plea for hep from the Europeans as opposed to a tortuous, and potentially dangerous, reliance on his sails for the return trip. True, they would probably help, but even the most benign scenario suggested that this would be at the cost of their intelligence crawling over the Free Canadian navy's most sophisticated weapons systems.

Another few minutes and we'll be amongst their tail, Sir, the tactical weapons director standing to his right noted tersely. He looked anxiously at his captain, clearly expecting some immediate response. *Let's start with the rear guard then and go for those two fat, lazy ones,* Lagard finally replied after a pause which seemed to reflect some considerable uncertainty. His finger jabbed on the screen at two large warships which were flanking either side of a couple of slow-moving ships at the American's rear. The latter appeared to be simple cargo vessels and for a moment he considered disregarding them *Probably broken down or two slow for the main body,* he concluded. Then Singh suggested that they might be carrying munitions or fuel, either of which would generate a useful explosion to interfere for the enemy's scanners. So it was that the focus La Cité's initial salvo was shifted from the two warships which were now joining the queue of vessels still edging their way into the mouth of The Straits.

Las Palmas

07.48 UTC April 3rd

How much more time do you need now? demanded Marie Jesu, the shrill tone of her voice indicative of the stimulants she had been dependent on for the past – how many days was it now? She could have slept of course, but the reality would have been that – given the situation – it would have been an attempt at sleep. The drill had been stopped yet again to add another string, giving Hansen and some of his team time to gulp down some hot RealCoffee which had magically appeared. The torrential rain had finally abated, but significantly the wind had fallen to an extent which now allowed all of the drilling rigs to come into operation.

Only a few minutes, Hansen replied, glancing at the image showing the position of the mass the Christians had deposited at the bottom of the shaft and the most up-to-date location of the drill head. *But you know this is one of the shallowest shafts? My men over there,* and he waved his hand to the north *are dealing with much deeper shafts. Unless we can find some additional drills, it will take the rest of the day.* He paused. *Unless, that is, you want to use explosives.*
Explosives? You can use them here? How they help? Marie Jesu, demanded, taking in this new possibility.
It helps by doing things quickly. If you think we have another day , we can continue drilling like now, Hansen replied with a weary smile. *If you are in a hurry to get these things out, we can weaken the concrete they have used to block the shafts with the shock from our explosions.*
And if you use too much?
If intelligence is right we get an early big bang - if we get it wrong. If we get it right, and he waved an arm in the direction of the sea *perhaps no big bang and no big splash.* Anna Maria laughed. The fatigue of not having slept for nearly forty eight hours was telling on her greatly, but the German's simplified English – about as much as she could cope with she admitted to herself- had its own hysterical humour. He certainly had an admirable, calm given their danger. *OK!* she almost shouted little bang to stop big splash. *We use*

explosives. You tell them. And she jerked a finger towards the ordnance team under their tarpaulin. Minutes later she found herself sitting in the shelter of the vacated tarpaulin doing something she had not done since her childhood. Praying.

Six thousand metres above the southern Huelva marshes.

07.59 UTC April 3rd

Henry knew that something was amiss from the behaviour of the crew, and from the fact that they had again come to a halt after what had appeared to him to be rather brief flight southwards. Though his field of vision was limited by the flight visors, the twitching of heads and incessant gesticulation was indicative of an almost tangible tension in the cabin. Looking at his watch had simply confirmed his suspicion that the launch of the aircraft had been delayed.

Finally, he could almost feel the release of tension as the flight crews clambered through the dirigible and opened the hatches leading into the aircraft cockpits. The cockpits sat relatively snug in specially designed bays in the dirigible but, despite this, there was a blast of freezing air as the hatch was opened. He shivered, momentarily shocked by the temperature change which penetrated even the insulation of his flight suit. *'Wouldn't like to have to bail out of this,'* he remarked to himself, and he made a momentary note to check what the temperature difference would be at the maximum altitude for these things. Almost immediately he abandoned the idea. *'They'll think I'm spying.'* he observed to himself. Even more surprising was that Marie-Claire was not one of the figures now easing themselves down into the aircraft cockpit. As though reading his thoughts, her voice suddenly broke in on his headphone to inform him that another of the pilots had been assigned a fighter this flight. She would remain in charge of the dirigible *...and him...* which he found both sensually suggestive and disturbing. Did she still have a fear that he would suddenly pull out a radio and contact London- or even worse the Americans- to inform of every non-secret he had learnt in recent days?

Henry had unthinkingly assumed that, as a pilot, she would fly an aircraft, and the issue of who would then fly the dirigible home had never occurred to him. Perhaps he would get an answer as to how such decisions were taken, though he could not detect from Marie-Claire's voice if she was relieved or irritated to have been deprived of this opportunity to engage the enemy directly. As soon as the pilots were in their seats, the cockpits were closed, hatch doors firmly sealed and the warning lights returning to their customary green to confirm the seals were intact.

The gunner immediately to his right turned. Henry assumed it was to look at himself, though neither could see through their visors. The gunner raised a thumb and then both hands, palm stretched outwards. It took Henry some time to realise that the wiggling fingers inside the gloves were counting down to something, and almost simultaneously the something revealed itself as the first fighter dropped clear of the dirigible pod. Unburdened, the dirigible lurched clumsily sideways and sickeningly skywards. *Didn't like the feel of that,* Henry mumbled to himself, trying to replace his stomach in its usual position.

The second comes soon, when that one is far enough away Marie-Claire's voice responded, reminding him that she controlled his communications within this precarious world and could monitor his every utterance. *It not very nice the first times, but it was a successful launch and the second- she will go in one minute. We have to work with the others. Coordinate as you say. Look out and you will see.*

Despite the restricted view, Henry immediately understood why she had made the suggestion. The sky was full of aircraft climbing steeply after their initial drop from the bellies of the dirigibles. Despite the variations in size and design, he surmised they must be fighters. On reflection, he found it strangely ironic that the European stars on their fuselages were such a source of comfort given the recent conflicts with his homeland – now, these star-bearing aircraft were the only barrier between the flimsy envelope in which he was sitting and the weapons on the cross-bearing American crafts. Must be trying to get a height advantage on the American aircraft, he decided after a further glance, confirming his earlier theory based on watching war films which had involved something about coming in '...*fast out of the morning sun....*'

Las Palmas

07.59 UTC April 3rd

ZR23D184 was not an inherently unstable mechanism. True, it would have been more reliable if Quality Control had not been so busy procreating behind that stack of crates on a hot Friday afternoon. If Quality Control had been doing his real job, he would have seen the unit drop and bounce on the concrete floor. Xintao Electronic Corporation's components were usually robust enough to cope with such misadventure, but the heavy sandal accidentally, but heavily, planted by one of its flustered employees had potentially been a step -literally- too far. True, it was a problem of the Corporation's own making. If pressures had been less, and penalties for mistakes less draconian, the worker involved would have honestly put the unit aside as a possible failure, and things would have developed differently. Such was not the case, and ZR23D184 was about to experience another shock.

The Straits of Gibraltar

08.00 UTC April 4th

Monroe and Smith were seated in the tactical warfare room on *Genesis,* busily congratulating themselves on the stupidity of the Europeans in delaying their attack, when the first missile attack was reported. The fleet's electronic surveillance systems had been watchful of the European dirigibles to the north west, which had appeared to be stationary and Monroe assumed they were awaiting instructions and reinforcements, and this was supported by the incoming data. Smith's explanation was simply that they are *Too fearful of the Lord's wrath to dare touch His chosen vessels.*

A limited air launch had already been achieved and two of Monroe's largest carriers had almost cleared The Straits and were preparing to launch their aircraft. This would create a growing air-defence shield, and every additional minute also meant more armed ships were entering the Mediterranean, many carrying with them a considerable increase in the armada's anti-aircraft capacity. If things remained unchanged, Monroe estimated that he would have parity with the enemy within twenty minutes and superiority within the half hour. By then, much of the armada should be nearing The Straits's eastern end or in the Mediterranean itself .

To say that news of a missile attack on the tail of his vast flotilla was a shock would have done no justice to the word. The sudden launch of a hostile salvo from what seemed to be within the fleet itself proved too much for Smith. Days of tension had frequently revealed what Monroe could only consider a fundamental instability in the President and now, to the horror of the surrounding crew, he sank to the deck in a crumpled heap. He was saved from further humiliation by Tuckman, who ordered the largest of the Presidential Guard to hoist Smith to his feet before he throwing him over his shoulders. On command from Tuckman they stormed out.

Such was their haste, that they failed to note the President's head colliding with a bulkhead - Smith's whimpering was immediately silenced. At another, time Monroe might have seized the opportunity for a quiet, treasonable, prayer that the blow had been fatal, but now he turned away, his

face ashen at the implications of the attack. A total disaster had been avoided by the prompt response of the destroyer commanders charged with protecting his key vessels, and the launch of a flurry of anti-missile missiles had succeeded in destroying one in-coming projectile and -it seemed- inflicting enough damage on another to avoid a successful detonation of its payload. This had not prevented a near miss on both *Omegas I and II,* and a direct hit on one of the nearby destroyers which exploded immediately, generating a huge fireball which threatened nearby vessels as its munitions blasted randomly from the burning hulk.
Monroe immediately concluded he was dealing with a potent foe– no light weapons could have ripped through one of his most modern ships. However, from his location near the front of the armada the mass of images from the vessels crowded in the narrow Straits made it impossible to identify the source of the attack. Frustrated by his inability to effectively direct operations, he snapped a series of orders to the captain of *Arkansas* to locate and destroy the attacker. He struggled to remember his name, gave up, and ended with an abrupt *Is that clear captain?*
Glancing again at his console, he ordered a further two destroyers towards the tail of the fleet to

reverse their course, but immediately regretted his decision as he was flooded with complaints from vessels narrowly avoiding collision as the warships attempted to turn in the congested passage. Torn between a desire to appear resolute, and the realisation that he had made a fundamental error, Monroe was about to countermand his order when news came of another wave of missiles penetrating the fleet's defences.

Whoever is doing this is good, he muttered, shocked at the speed with which his unidentified assailant had been able to launch a second strike. Then the shocking thought suddenly struck him that he might be dealing with more than one attacker. '*What if there were more? What if Smith had been correct in his fears of treachery and disloyal crews were using the situation to their advantage?*' he demanded of himself. There was only one way to resolve this. Turning again to the bridge's tactical warfare display, he made a swift calculation that the first flight launched to engage the Europeans could be diverted. If he ordered his aircraft west now, they would be able to hunt down and destroy the hostile wolves amongst his flock. True, his vanguard's cover would be weakened, but other aircraft would be in the air as soon as the next carrier entered calmer waters. He had just given the order when Tuckman swung his huge frame

through the door and, without the slightest trace of respect, barked *The President wants so see you immediately Admiral.*
Monroe hesitated. This was not time to leave his command, but neither was it time to further irritate Smith. Lurking at the back of Monroe's mind for several minutes now, had been the name of the principle ship charged with protecting the two *Omega* vessels - *Arkansas*, one of a minority of warships without a religious connotation. Monroe had selected this and another three destroyers on the basis of the quality of both the vessels and their commanders, but as soon the attacks started the fear had gripped him that Smith might seize upon this as an explanation for their misfortune. This would explain Tuckman's demeanour. *'Here we go again,'* was the only polite expression passing through Monroe's mind as he relinquished command to the ship's captain, and trudged wearily down the corridor in Tuckman's wake.

20 miles north, north east of Tarfaya
08.02 UTC April 3rd

The N1 was a poor, rutted descendent of a once relatively good link between Morocco and what had been Mauritania; but then there had been no meaningful trade between the two areas for years. Yes, some trade in weapons and slaves, but nothing that either feeble government would consider worth spending scarce money on. Adams and his men were experiencing this reality first hand, their vehicles screeching, jolting and jumping along the road at a speed which was some three to four times greater than would be considered by any sane individual. Sanity was not the issue, for whilst Adams was unique in his command in knowing the precise nature of their mission, he could not, would not, attempt to hide his fear from the men in his own vehicle. He constantly, nervously glanced at his watch, double checking its time with others and hanging over the vehicle's edge to look backwards as though to catch sight of.... Of what?

Thanks to the wonders of electronic communication, the concern and gossip spread from helmet to helmet down the convoy of ten vehicles speeding behind in his dust. As rumour always breeds on uncertainty, the rumours were numerous and variable. Those immediately around him had assumed that he was fearful of pursuit from Tarfaya, though what there could be to fear coming from that stinking hole raised a number of eye brows. Most widely accepted was the variant which saw Adams as fearful of pursuit by a large, but hitherto unseen, garrison issuing from Tarfaya to avenge the Christian's affront to their community. A very small number, those sharing fundamentalist religious convictions and most fertile minds, were of the conviction that Adams had somehow been involved in an attempt to exorcise the devil amongst the WUCCIES on Las Palmas, the attempt had somehow failed, and that he was now fearful that the Devil himself might pursue them until they reached the benevolent protection of President Smith, God's Holy Prophet, and their beloved Brothers and Sisters in the main fleet.

Oblivious of the extent of this wild speculation, at a more mundane level two smashed front teeth were the price Adams had already paid for the price for the quality of the road and of urging his driver to pelt along with no consideration for damage to machine or person. An unexpectedly savage lurch, had smashed his face onto the shell of the amphibian, was a direct result. Disregarding the blood dripping from his mouth, it became increasingly clear that Adams's newly developed fascination with both his watch and a detailed map of the area was simply linked to a desire to gain height and distance from the ocean. Both seemed to be elusive.

It had crossed Adams's mind that he had been a fool to have chosen to travel north. South towards El

Aaiun was doubtless safer if his calculations were in any way flawed, but his choice had been made in the heated minutes of their arrival and there was no way he was going to take his men back through what would now be at least a vengeful and prepared enemy to their south - and at worst? It was an academic discussion anyway he concluded. There simply wasn't time to change routes now. He glanced again at his watch and then at the road. True, they were slowly climbing and the distance from the coast growing, but even his firm convictions in the power of The Lord did not extend to provoking divine support needlessly. A few more miles would be a true blessing and the map showed the road bending further away from the coast towards the south east and climbing slowly – hopefully enough to offer safety.

Las Palmas

08.03 UTC April 3rd

Anna Maria found herself choking in the swirling cloud of pulverised ash which Hansen's explosion had thrown over the exhausted teams still assembled on the peak of Caldera de Taburiente. It was difficult to identify individual figures, but Hansen's height made him immediately recognisable and there was something about the way he strode towards her which invoked the slightest stirrings of hope. *That went well!* he roared. *Our explosion fractured the American concrete in the shaft and we can access from the side with the hole me made. Now we will use this*, and he gestured towards one of the hoist which had been sitting idly until then, to pull it out *and then we can get to what is below.*

So how many shafts have you cleared? she demanded, her curtness revealing profound fatigue. *And how long before we get to the bottom of them all?*

This was the first one and I don't know. Depends on the concrete they have used, was Hansen's matter-of- fact response, and he lopped off to re-join his men.

Probably too little too late, Anna Maria mused, *but we can only do our best and ....* She stopped the train of thought at that juncture as her head filled with the multitude of lectures her father had given her in her youth using that same expression.

Six thousand metres above CadizWall
08.03 UTC April 3rd

Rather than respecting the order to maintain general radio silence, the communication channels had become a pan-European forum questioning the logic in delaying the attack. The general consensus was that some important military figure – some said the Commander in Chief himself – had wanted to be involved in the action, and that this had been the cause of the delay. Others claimed that it had been decided that there were inadequate European aircraft to counter the American's might, a suggestion immediately refuted by the consensus that it was simple madness to allow more Christian ships into the calm waters where they could launch their fighters. There was even a rumour that a squadron of submarines were even now bearing down on the enemy to wreak havoc and sink their key capital ships, though there appeared to be a total lack of certainty as to whether the Confederation possessed any submarines and, if so, where they were based. The latter theory received short shrift - unless the submarines were invisible to their comrades' own electronic scanning systems.

The unanimous feeling was that lives and aircraft would be lost as a result of the delays and that there was almost certainly a political game being played at a high level between those fearful of the consequences of engaging with Smith and those fearful of not engaging. It was, in Marie-Claire's opinion, typical Euro-political cultural clashes at play, and it was all the more academic since the Canadian ship had attacked Smith's rear.

At this height and distance, Marie-Claire's radar was adequate to give a detailed view of La Cité's attack and its consequences. There had been a clear command to avoid either engaging with the

Canadian vessel, or to take any action which might be deemed hostile, consequently she had found herself mulling over the strategy of the ship's commander and asking the fundamental question as to whether suicidal tendencies or strategic brilliance was guiding his hand.

Strategic logic told Marie-Claire that the Christian Americans were illogically leaving their tail vulnerable and wasting valuable capital ships in the defence of two decrepit cargo vessels. Her deeper probes had revealed that they were not carrying passengers – her first theory- and if anything appeared to be very lightly crewed. Their slow progress was, she had initially assumed, indicative that the vessels might be experiencing mechanical difficulties, but this explanation had been immediately abandoned when they had demonstrated a surprising turn of speed when the Canadians had launched their first attack. There was something not quite right about the situation, and her natural caution had resulted in a request for a more sophisticated scan from one of the intelligence drones to her east. That would take some time.

For now, the chaos generated by two Christian destroyers attempting to reverse their course in the middle of their own fleet intrigued her; their apparent task being one that could more easily be achieved by other ships in the vicinity. Forgetting this, her attention was suddenly focused on a change in the flight pattern of several squadrons of American fighters which had initially appeared to be engaged in an eastwards sortie and were now flying westwards towards her. Whether their target was Marie-Claire's dirigible squadrons or the Canadian vessel was unclear, but she was unwilling to wait while events unfolded - and even less inclined to leave the single vessel with no air support. Each dirigible in her command still had one fighter aboard and, after a brief conversation with her commanding officer, she ordered her squadron to start deploying interceptors between the approaching American aircraft and the Canadian vessel.

The Straits of Gibraltar
08.04 UTC April 3rd

Monroe halted immediately when the sirens on *Genesis* started to scream. Even Tuckman stopped and hesitated for a second, the question clearly passing through his brain –Monroe believed he had a brain, though probably of the asinine sort if that were not too insulting to asses – *'Who had done that if Monroe was here with him?'* Monroe's immediate reaction was to turn and hurry back to regain command, but there was something in Tuckman's face – and was there the slightest movement of his hand to the holster on his hip?- which combined with a sense of fatigue to allow him to meekly continue along the passageway to Smith's cabin. Smith's personal physician hurtled past, choosing to push Monroe to the side rather than Tuckman. Monroe noted the gesture, itself an indication of evolving political power, but of more immediate concern was the realisation that this would involve even further delay. The slightest mistake with Smith's health could cost the doctor his own life, so Smith would be examined with extreme meticulousness.

Listen, he said, turning to Tuckman, *can I come back when The President is feeling better? I feel I should be at my station at a time like this,* and he waved a hand in the air as though it would make something concrete from the wailing of the sirens. The confidence he placed in his officers was rapidly being replaced by a growing concern that His beloved fleet was under attack and he was not at his post. True, they were good, loyal men and women, but the majority had only limited combat experience and Monroe sensed that fighting in the Straits's confines would test their limits.

The President wants to see you immediately and so he shall, was Tuckman's inevitable reply. *The doctor will not be overly long.*

But it's crucial that I resume command! Monroe found himself shouting, realising immediately that he had committed a cardinal error.

My orders are to take you to The President instantly, Tuckman barked. His face had clouded with anger, masking any false goodwill it had contained, and there was a heavy emphasis on *'instantly'. We can trust on The Lord and the quality of our crews can we not Admiral? After all, it was you who chose and trained them - no?* Monroe immediately recognised the lethal potential of the question. There was no point in arguing that Smith had, on a simple whim, frequently replaced good officers with poorer people of his own choice. Sometimes it was a feeling – justified or otherwise – that there was a lack of loyalty to himself or The Cause or both.

There was also jealousy. However close officers had been to The President, most inevitably grew closer to Monroe and developed an unreserved respect for his military and leadership capacities. Not that they dared voice this shift, for Tuckman's agents would find out, make note and ensure that he had the information to poison Smith when the need arose. Whether it was Smith or Tuckman who was the true

President was a question that Monroe had started to ask himself, but Tuckman's ability to command loyalty amongst his agents and the Presidential Guard was not subject to debate. *Shall we?* the man demanded. Monroe realised that he had been standing in silence, deep in thought, for several seconds. He sighed and, resigned for now, shuffled along the passageway with his head bowed and hands deep in his pockets.

Six thousand metres, twenty kilometres south east of CadizWall.

08.06 UTC April 3rd

Strictly speaking, European dirigibles were classified as transports rather than combat craft, though they were not to be totally under-estimated. In addition to two long-distance, high velocity machine guns manned by gunners, each craft carried a pair of long-range, air-to-air missiles and a collection of interceptors and defensive systems intended to disrupt incoming missile. In addition, each wing had its own, small, escort of fighters which were kept stowed until needed. Not that anyone would deny that the dirigibles were inherently vulnerable. Lacking speed and the ability to climb swiftly, the essence of survival was to either destroy enemy aircraft at a distance or keep them at a distance. Failing that, a final, desperate avenue to safety was to use the on-board gases to climb to an altitude beyond the limits of most fighters. Such an action placed enormous strains on the crafts and crews, taking them to- and potentially beyond- the oxygen and heating systems' design limits. As Marie-Claire's squadron swung into position at the far end of The Straits, she was reminded that her instructor had always advised trainee pilots to remember the final option which, despite its own inherent risks, he considered this a neat trick to use when the alternative was being turned into a blazing, fifty - metre - long torch which would plunge to the ground.

The on-board systems now provided a detailed image of the battle developing at the eastern end of The Straits. The Christians had been able to launch a full three squadrons before the first European aircraft arrived. There had been considerable concern amongst the crews as to how their aircraft would compare with the Americans. In the last conflict, the old U.S.A.F. technical superiority had been – with a few minor exceptions- overwhelming. She suspected that the attack had been delayed to ensure numerical superiority in the hope that this would compensate for an assumed American technical superiority. Since the last conflicts however, the Confederation had ploughed considerable resources into improving its defences and, judging from the communications chatter and the early destruction of a number of enemy aircraft, there was a growing sense that either the Americans were using inferior craft or crews, or that research and development had paid off. Already, the first attack was being pressed home against ships at the American vanguard, several of which had already been damaged.

Almost directly ahead of her, and slightly to her east, she could physically see the Canadian warship as a tiny dot on the ocean. Apparently as a symbol of mutual trust, the ship had opened parts of its communications and electronic systems so that it could interface with the Europeans. The information gleaned revealed a potent fighting machine which had already delivered four missile salvos into the American fleet. The Canadian captain was using a simple strategy of chewing into Monroe's rear by taking out identified warships and disregarding troop carriers and lightly armed vessels which he deemed posed no immediate threat. Until now, his success had been at least partly reliant on an element of surprise and the sheer volume of traffic whose electronic haze and
multiple radar images would doubtless be hindering attempts to locate the attacker.

Such was the confusion she was now witnessing, that Marie-Claire found herself wondering if the American warships attempting to back-track through the waterway would successfully navigate it without colliding with their only vessels. She considered whoever had ordered the operation a fool - time and resources would have been better spent driving forward into the Mediterranean where space would be on the American's side.

Her immediate focus was on the rapid approach of twelve Christian aircraft which posed a potential threat to both the Canadian vessel and her own command. She was astonished to see that, rather than seek flexibility by moving out into open waters, the Canadian response to the in-coming danger was to move at full speed into the tightly packed rear of the fleet, simultaneously opening fire with its full range of surface-to-surface armaments. The rapid approach of their own warships further deprived the Christian ships of navigation room and, in the growing chaos, what little order there had been started to dissolve as individual captains attempted to save their own vessels at the expense of those around them.

They really made someone very angry, she commented to her co-pilot, gesticulating in the general direction of La Cité. *Look at all the aircraft they are wasting on this.*

They need them at the front. But he is clever this captain. If he is with their own ships it will be more difficult for them to target im. But when they do, he will be in big trouble. For now, we can help. For no logical reason 'help' triggered something in her memory. Glancing back, she saw the English man huddled miserably in his seat. *Why was he brought along*? she demanded of herself. *Ah yes, an order in case he tried to make contact with ...? And were the English still an enemy? Or had he been brought along to die? Certainly that would be a good end for the bitch woman.'* and for a moment she tried to remember where she had been ordered. *enri* she spoke clearly into her mouthpiece *make sure you keep your body armour and helmet in place. Things may not be good now,* and to her own surprise she turned and blew him a symbolic kiss from the outside of her visor.

Chapter XI
Inherent instability
Las Palmas
08.06 UTC April 3rd

ZR23D184 had not been an inherently unstable mechanism until the trauma of its experience in the Sino-Nigerian factory, but that and several years of less than careful handling had been capped by the shock of Hansen's explosion some minutes earlier. Not that a non-sentient piece of silicon based electronics had the emotional framework to be affected by such things. ZR23D184 was not, after all, one of the sentient, evolving systems which had been under development before the religious and climatic – Henry had always preferred 'climatic and religious' – wars had brought such peripheral things to an end.

But the shock of the explosion had been too much. Encased in concrete at the base of the first shaft that Adams and his men had dug, ZR23D184's response was to malfunction. Not all malfunctions are, of course, inherently serious and their seriousness may be very case specific. On this occasion, the response was to lose chronology – seconds were no longer respected as fixed units of time but random units as time leapt forward in bites until the magic time of 08.33 was reached.

The serious implications of this particular malfunction were instantly apparent to Hansen, Anna Maria and their teams, still labouring to crack the concrete encasements at the bottom of Adams's shafts. The first manifestation was a searing blast of energy, instantly killing the squad working around its mouth. Almost simultaneously, there was a thrusting upwards of the rock surface as though the stresses of the planet were focused solely on that limited point of the earth's surface. The upward surge threw Anna Maria off her feet, flinging her against the charred remnants of an abandoned Christian half-truck. Despite the pain and shock of the impact, she felt an instant wave of relief. Intelligence had warned of something truly momentous, of an event which would threaten the entire island and those living far beyond. Either they had been misinformed, or the Americans had failed.

The euphoria and relief dissipated as, using the vehicle as a prop, she pulled herself up-right and immediately noted an odd sensation in her stomach. She was back in her childhood and the times when she had inflicted repeated big dipper rides on her unfortunate parents. There was that same feeling of rushing upwards and then leaving one's stomach in a different place when reaching the top of the ride and dropping down amidst the screams of the riders and the rumbles and vibrations of the car. She could picture it all in her mind, and with it the times in later years when she had used the pseudo –fear as an excuse to hug the boy she was later to marry and bear children for. Suddenly, she realised that her stomach had stopped going up and was now being left in space as it used to be when she reached the peak of the ride, and there was the same grinding and rumbling and swaying as there had been on the old cars.

Still stunned by the force of the explosion, she climbed hesitantly to her feet amidst the swirling dust, struggling to understand the events unfolding around her. Fatigue, following days of constant action against the Americans, helped emphasise her initial, total bemusement as, for the first time in her twenty or so adult years on the island, she became aware of a large cliff looming out of the swirling dust. The cliff's history was writ large in the thick soil strata, each competing with its neighbours in terms of darkness. Alarm followed bemusement as she realised that the cliff was growing, its increase in height coinciding with the mounting rumbles from the big dipper upon which she had imagined herself seated minutes earlier. Initially she failed to notice the horror on Hansen's face as he too managed to struggle to his feet, then it dawned on her that his bulging eyes were focused on something behind her, a something which was clearly growing in stature if the focus of his eyes were to be trusted. For the first time she also became aware of a persistent movement of air which had now gained sufficient strength to lift her soil-caked hair.

Turning confused her further. Where there had been no cliff, there was now a face of some hundreds of metres towering above her. Where there had been horizon, there was now only sea, but a sea growing with every part-second that passed. Finally, came the horrifying realisation that it was the land upon which she was standing which was grinding its way down the big dipper of her childhood. At the bottom was no shallow pool designed to splash the screaming, excited occupants of the car. Seconds later, all memories and confusion were extinguished as the first of millions of tons of Atlantic water crashed down upon her.

Best laid plans

08.06 UTC April 3rd

Adams's plan had been one of great simplicity. He had a love of old films, so popular in the late twentieth century, in which teams of – often heroically doomed- astronauts had been launched into space to save an impure earth from potential destruction as an asteroid hurled into it. For him, the planet's repeated salvation had missed the key message- that human kind should repent before God himself punished a sinful earth by allowing homo sapiens to follow the vast majority of dinosaurs into extinction.

Whether the demise of the latter had been an indication of an earlier sinfulness was something which had occasionally troubled him, and he had grappled with the issue for many years. It had been finally resolved when he had – clearly through God's divine guidance- once drifted into a discussion of the issue whilst interrogating a captured pastor from the Federal army. The woman would have been executed eventually regardless, but the sophistication of her arguments, including the issues of sinfulness and redemption in which she had used dinosaurs as an example, that he had taken it upon himself to execute her on the spot. As a junior officer, he had been forced to justify his actions by arguing that the pastor's powers of persuasion were indicative of her close link with the devil – perhaps the devil incarnate? The argument had not impressed his captain and Adams had foreseen potential demotion and transfer to a forward combat unit. Then, fortuitously, Smith's summons had arrived and Adams subsequently enjoyed publicly lambasting and humiliating the same captain, secure in the knowledge that he was in President Smith's favour.

There was nothing philosophical in the events which Adams had now unleashed. The potential instability of The Canaries had been considered and re-considered in geological studies for over a hundred years, and the potential for parts to collapse violently into the Atlantic was one which had attracted considerable attention in specialist circles. The probability of such an event at any point of time was perhaps as remote was the likelihood of an asteroid strike on the earth, but asteroid defence had been much more attractive as a justification for spending to the American Congress by the military and defence sector. Adams's proposal to Smith was indeed one which had been considered by various terrorist groups, and for years the area had been under American intelligence surveillance. But interest, and possibly knowledge, had been lost amidst the general economic and military decline which had slid into a general global fracturing filled overtly, or latently, with hostile political and religious groupings.

There was, therefore, no originality in the ideas Adams had stumbled across in reading the old *National Geographic. It* was, therefore, no more than the resurrection – so aptly called by Smith – of an old hypothesis in which a catastrophic failure on the fault line on Cumbre Vieja would result in millions of tons of soil and rocks cascading into the sea and so creating a tidal wave. Most of the theory held that it would be the eastern seaboard of the United States which would suffer most, and Adams had spent months with colleagues modelling various scenarios in order to ensure that maximum damage would be focused on WUCCIE-held land. A little further computer modelling had tweaked the collapse so that the resulting wave would have a more northerly direction. However, because there could be no complete certainty that the model would be replicated in the real world, as a precaution Smith had convinced a compliant Grand Council to move all Souls who could not initially be transported to New Eden to transfer to the safety of higher ground in the west.

The subsequent decision to move the Christian Republic's seat to the Holy Land had been rubber-stamped by The Grand Council of Thirteen. The plan had been revealed by God to Smith and any opposition had been silenced by the trial and execution for heresy of a key opponents who had dared to question Smith's revelation. Details of the plan were, of course, kept secret outside The Grand

Council, though preparations inevitably generated many rumours.

One contained an element of truth in that factions in Smith's inner circle had urged him to respond to pleas for assistance from zealous Zionists who had been driven from Jerusalem by a combined force of liberal Jews and Muslims. As in America, economic stresses in the old Middle East had tended to generate increasing tensions between ultra-religious and secular and liberal groups or all persuasions. For decades there had been shifting alliances between radical Christian fundamentalist and some Zionist elements, and those closest to Smith were continually interpreting the Old Testament as containing references associating his leadership and the need to create a new Judeo-Christian state to confront liberal and moderate Islamic opposition. It was not by chance that Smith called his military 'crusaders'.

Adams's plan had been one of great simplicity and had immediately appealed to Smith who, as a man of great simplicity, would never have accepted the substantial bribes in gold and precious minerals which rumour claimed had been offered as an inducement to his delivering the might of the Christian fleet to ultra-orthodox factions. If the dead were capable of consolation, Anna Maria,

Hansen and their teams might have gained some consolation that this simplicity had now been lost. The complexity in Adams's plan had been in the timing of the series of explosions which would both ensure the western flank of the island sheered away and that the resulting colossal displacement of ocean would have a slight northerly twist to the tsunami he planned to generate. The premature, and uncoordinated, explosions initiated by ZR23D184444 failed to deliver the critical mass projected in the calculations. Faced with the fundamental inertia of the Atlantic waters, the strength of a largely opposing wind, and the initial void generated by the collapsing island, the tsunami's crest hesitated some thirty kilometres from its source, folded, and then collapsed back in itself, gathering speed as the waters poured back towards The Canaries and the Moroccan coast.

Altitude six thousand metres, twenty five kilometres south east of Cadiz wastes. 08.11 UTC April 3rd

Marie-Claire's on-board warfare systems were busy analysing the threats developing to her east. The enemy's rapidly approaching aircraft would soon be a threat to her squadron, and theoretically she should already have ordered all the escort aircraft launched to engage them. However, intuitively she still felt there was something wrong. If her systems were correct, the Americans had not even troubled to try and penetrate her own battle capabilities. Attacking military software was fundamental in any conflict and she found it unbelievable that this had not been attempted or that they had detailed knowledge of the latest European designs. So, they were being either unbelievably arrogant or their total focus on the Canadian vessel indicated a pathological hatred of its temerity in daring to attack. Or, the thought crept into her mind, could it be there was a concern that the Canadian ship posed a threat to something of great value. But what was it?

Look! She was brought back to the immediate concerns by her navigator, who had taken the co-pilot's seat after the first launch. She looked across at the display to which he was gesticulating. Heating had been cut to increase their flight time and the screen was partly obscured by his thick gloves. Marie-Claire's immediate fear was that she would witness bad news. In the first conflict between the Confederation and the Americans years of under-investment had resulted in such an imbalance in military capability that the Europeans had almost immediately been forced to sue for peace. Since then, huge resources had been allocated to improving the Confederation's military and this appeared to be showing results. The screen revealed the deadly dance to her south east between Confederation and American aircraft. Those who had witnessed the first conflict had reported that it was simply a matter of the Confederation's aircraft being blasted from the sky. Now, if anything, the enemy's red were slowly being obliterated, while the screen filled green dots representing the arrival of more of her own aircraft. *We are doing well? No?* one of the gunners demanded, having picked up on the exchanges in the cockpit.

Ye, we are doing well, she replied, lifting her visor long enough to beam reassuringly at her crew seated along the long, dimly lit tube which was the dirigible. The cold, oxygen-poor air hit her instantly and she hesitated only long enough to ensure everyone had seen her before she rapidly slid the visor back. She made a special point of including Henry who appeared to be cowering further into his seat. '*Yes we are doing well – for now'* she found herself thinking ' *but we are only dealing with a minute part of their might.* Then, looking at the aircraft rapidly approaching her position, she reluctantly acknowledged that she had to launch her own aircraft both to assist La Cité and to ensure that her dirigibles were not left exposed to the Christian fighters. *Our fuel reserves for the year,* she found herself mumbling before giving the order to launch. *Vincenzo, you ok to take it this time? You have much experience with this model, no?*

Si. She's a good bird to go play with the Yankees. With no further ado he unplugged his oxygen tube, attached it to the reserve tank on his suit, slipped from the co-pilot's seat, and waddled as quickly as his suit would permit to the dock holding the last of the three aircraft they had been carrying.

The Straits

08.11 UTC April 3rd

Monroe could feel *Genesis* vibrating and the rolls diminishing as the ship pushed forward at top speed into the open, calmer, Mediterranean. He could also feel the occasional shudder and muffled wush as a missile was launched and the unmistakable chatter or anti-aircraft fire. In frustration, he bit his lip viciously, the blood trickling sufficiently profusely to attract the attention of one of the Presidential Guard. Momentarily, Monroe found his reaction interesting. There was a split second of panic – '*Has the Admiral poisoned himself on my shift?* perhaps – followed by another second or so of empathy as their eyes met and Monroe flashed what was intended to be a reassuring glance. Then stern distance re-established itself as Tuckman glanced back from his role as Smith's arch-comforter and the guard remembered the dangers of fraternising with someone who, whilst admiral of the fleet, could be branded a presidential enemy at any second.

For Monroe it was momentarily reassuring to know that there was latent sympathy even at this level, though its practical benefits were doubtful. It was bad – very bad- to find that *Genesis* – and assumedly other ships – were being forced to defend themselves at this juncture. Whether this was through superior numbers or equipment was irrelevant- what was important was that his defences were being challenged. It was yet another decision by Smith, this time to refuse to prioritise the passage of the aircraft carriers, which would now be limiting their options. Suddenly Smith opened his eyes. Until then they had been clenched shut, as if in pain, intense prayer, or through a desire to shut out the reality surrounding him. Gently, he pushed Tuckman aside and beckoned Monroe towards him.

Western end of The Straits
08.11 UTC April 3rd

Despite the incessant drills of the past few days, and the sophistication of its systems, La Cité's defences were struggling to counter the combined threat from both American aircraft and ships. Lagard had feared this from the time they had sailed from the eastern coast, knowing that the ships had been little more than a floating guardian of the St. Lawrence approaches and that the majority of its crew possessed enthusiasm but lacked experience. He had attempted to compensate for this with repeated drills during their crossing, including sounding battle stations in the depth of the night in order to test responses to the full. Despite this, the strain was showing on the weapons teams as they struggled to respond to the target-rich environment. *Target rich* was a splendidly euphemistic term – each target actually having the potential to obliterate La Cité and its crew.

Lagard's weapons officers had already identified that part of the problem lay in the software's lack of a protocol with which to distinguish between the hostile American aircraft and the first of the European fighters which were attempting to intercept them. These were problems in adapting the battle software within such a limited time, and his team had been forced to resolve the problem by individually tagging each European aircraft as 'safe' during their approach. This manual solution was extremely cumbersome and the inherent lack of goodwill was already evident in a tense argument underway with a European flight leader as to whether it was La Cité or American fire which had downed two of his aircraft. Miraculously, not a single ordinance had hit La Cité so far and the crew were elated at the destruction they had been able to inflict. Lagard had ordered that fire be concentrated on what were more obviously warships, and no fewer than three capital ships and a half dozen or so other vessels had been damaged or sunk. One must have been carrying aviation fuel or munitions given the force with which it exploded and sank immediately upon being hit.

Now, the advantage of surprise had been lost and he was facing a more organized and determined attack bearing down on him from the east. Whatever the relative quality of systems and crews, he was dooming his own command by continuing the fight here. Though he could not out-run the Christian aircraft, he could allow his defences to concentrate on them by out-running the surface threat, and La Cité's prospects of survival had been greatly increased by the European aircraft flying southwards. He reluctantly reversed course and was making full speed north westwards into the Atlantic. *Better to survive today and join with the Federal American fleet,* he informed his crew.

Altitude thirty thousand metres. Thirty kilometres west of Cadiz wastes 08.29 UTC April 3rd

The Intelligence Corp battle computers were mounted on dirigibles over four times the size of Marie-Claire's own. Designed to be stationed at the highest possible altitude, and the greatest distance, in an attempt to minimise the risk of attack, they bristled with the best technology the Confederation could muster. Consequently, within seconds Adams's small nuclear blast in the Canaries had been identified as such, and a team given the responsibility for monitoring the area.

This, the first ever use of a nuclear device in Confederation territory, represented a major game change, and Marie-Claire's launch of her defensive aircraft was immediately aborted as frenzied consultations followed with Central Command. There were still several minutes before the nearest American aircraft posed an immediate threat to her squadron, and the launch of any aircraft was a serious issue. Valuable crews and aircraft, had been lost in the past through the fiasco of having to eject over Wastelands outside government control because of lack of a landing strip or insufficient fuel. The latter was so precious as to limit any launching without good cause, and this far south the aircraft already in combat would stretch the local bases to their limits.

For now, the Christian squadrons sent against La Cité had been halted. They had lost nearly a quarter of their numbers for the loss of some ten percent of the numerically similar European aircraft. Marie-Claire's initial reaction was that this was an indication of a good return on the investment since the last conflict, but there was something in the chatter between the pilots which left her feeling distinctly uneasy. Not only were there regular comments about the smoke being ejected from the Christian engines- sure sign of either age or shortage of access to quality fuel- but the odd comment about these being old models. '*Was it possible that the Christian commander was testing 'her' forces? Were these the best the Christians had stolen from the old U.S.A.F.? Or were they simply expendable?*' These unresolved questions troubled her deeply as they did the Intelligence Corp when she raised her concerns.

Attempting to juggle the stream of data coming from the diverse stages around her, the thought suddenly struck her that far too much Christian effort and too many sacrifices had been made, both at sea and in the air, in shielding the two vessels which had lagged behind at the very rear of their fleet. '*We need to have another look at the contents of these two* ,' she mused, sensing once again that there was something '*not-quite-right*' .

A distance of some twenty miles now separated these anomalies from the main fleet and, as if to confirm her suspicions, the skeleton crew of the two vessels suddenly abandoned them using a flotilla of fast boats. Their passage took them close to the warships which had been pursuing La Cité and for one this proved a fatal error; the boat offering a soft, quick target for a Confederation aircraft at the end of an unsuccessful attack against a Christian destroyer. These had also dramatically, puzzlingly, changed course. They were no longer attempting to engage with the Canadian vessel, but had reversed course and were now sailing at what seemed to be maximum speed to re-join the main fleet. *There is something wrong* she virtually shouted to the empty chair at her side. *What so important about those vessels that they were being protégé in this way?* The latter question was directed to her own intelligence. Without waiting for a reply, she ordered her own systems to perform a detailed scan of the two ships. Any potential reply from her own command was suddenly blocked as an American-sounding voice boomed in her helmet. The European communication command chain had evolved to deal with a number of –not always- positive realities. First amongst these was a bizarre reliance on various forms of English as the unifying strand in communications between Confederation forces. Secondly, was the need to consult and reconcile differences between different –sometimes differing – military and political cultures. The resulting command chain was such that strategic decisions were normally jointly considered by whichever senior officer was not immediately involved in a combat role and the senior intelligence officer on duty. Whenever possible, data was simultaneously relayed to the air command centre in Munich, but here lay the third weakness in the absence of robust satellite and terrestrial relays. So far south, there was no certainty of a reliable link.

It seemed that temporarily she was the most senior, local officer not involved in direct combat operations - and so the communication from the American-speaker had come directly to her. *Command* MAC 7 9, the voice boomed again, using her personal call sign, *this is Lagard, captain of the Free Canada cruiser La Cité du Quebec. Please to confirm communication channel and access to your battle computers.*

Marie-Claire hesitated. She was initially cautious that this might prove to be a trick, but then she considered the improbability of the Americans having accessed her own command code. *Your reasons captain?* she replied, trying to hide her caution behind a friendly tone. Sharing general intelligence

with the Canadians was within her orders, but she had no orders to allow them access to the actual battle computers themselves. This was another, much more serious, matter.
The reply was immediate. *Command MAC 7 9. I need information about hostile disposition and.....* There was a sudden break in the communication, the silence filled by the hiss typical of an open channel. *This one is more decisive than our commanders,* Marie-Claire muttered to herself, though she reflected that the hatred felt by the Free Canadians towards the Christians had been legendary since the slaughter of the Toronto militia. Turning to her screens, the reason for the communications break was immediately clear. For the first time a Christian fighter had managed to evade both Confederation and Canadian capabilities, the blast caused by its missiles clearly glowing orange near La Cité stern. *'The damage must be quite grave'*, she immediately concluded. It was a tribute to the ability of the Canadian crew that they had managed to intercept so much incoming fire until now, and Marie-Claire felt a sudden wave of sympathy for the ship's commander. *'How and why has he found himself so far from home?'* she demanded of herself
You still there captain? the link suddenly re-connected. *Before those bastards so rudely interrupted I was saying that*

y orders are to harry these maniacs while I still have the ability, but we have done all we can for now and I'm not seeing my crew massacred pour rien. But I am totally blind to the west – either jamming or technical issues. Can you give me data for that area? And another question. We have something much to the south at the very edge of our systems. Wondered if that was anything to do with our Christian friends. They were down there earlier. You know that? Was it another nuclear bomb?

I knew that there was something, she replied instantly, certain that there were no security implications *but I have nothing sure on what is happening there. For your request, I shall have to confirm. Please wait some minutes. OK? Please wait,* and she closed the link with the hope that the conversation had been monitored by the intelligence dirigibles.

She was disappointed. There was silence for several vital seconds before a junior officer opened a channel and told her that the system was busy dealing with urgent calls. She was about to demand greater priority for her own request when he abruptly closed the channel, leaving her fuming. Reliant on her own information, she turned to the tactical battle screens. With the exception of the two stragglers and the warships sent to engage La Cité, the last of the American fleet was starting to clear The Straits. Of the group sent to attack La Cité,

one ship was burning fiercely whilst the other was attempting the seemingly impossible by simultaneously sailing eastwards at high speed whilst trying to shield the remaining boats from the abandoned freighters. It was obvious to her that there was no overall coordination between the vessels and this was almost immediately confirmed as one of the inflatable vessel made the mistake of crossing a cruiser's bows and was immediately sliced in two. '*They are panicking,*' Marie-Claire thought to herself, '*but why?*'
What is happening? The demand came from one of the pilots who had taken up position in the fighters slung below the dirigible With the aircraft engines inactive, and with no heating from the dirigible systems, the crews were sitting in the confines of freezing cockpits. The convention was that aircraft were launched almost immediately the crew were in place, indeed there could be a relatively narrow window in which the pilots would avoid hypothermia, but in the confusion she had forgotten her earlier order to prepare for launch. Before she could reply, Henry suddenly lumbered into sight and back into her consciousness. She had forgotten of his existence as an increasingly miserable lump slumped in a seat far behind her, and silently cursed the idiots who had ordered her to bring him along

for no reason she could fathom. She re-established his link and silent thoughts turned to vocal abuse as she cursed him as an idiot who had not fully emptied his bladder before launch and now wanted to know how to pee while wearing a complete battle suit. The comedy broke the immediate and the crew could be seen rolling with laughter while Henry stood, clearly trying to control his natural urges with his hands, begging pitifully for information.

The comedy ended dramatically as simultaneously the Canadian's voice filled her helmet and the alarms on the tactical computers burst into life. Temporarily distracted, they had failed to notice that two of the enemy's fighters had broken free from the main battle and were powering towards them . Whether the manoeuvre was in desperation to escape the conflict, or an attack upon the dirigible squadron, was irrelevant - the dirigibles were hopelessly vulnerable in close combat so all hostile aircraft had to be kept at maximum range. Disregarding the strident demands from La Cité's captain, she hesitated, thinking of the most appropriate armaments to use when two long-range missiles detached from a dirigible to her port. *Merde Lieutenant Vasos! You wait for orders or you go back to training*, she shouted, irritated by the lack of discipline- though she would have chosen the same weapons. No sooner had the missiles dropped well clear of the dirigible, their red silhouettes clearly outlined against the clear morning sky, than their engines ignited. Propelled forward, they spat orange flames as they curved away on diverging trajectories dictated by their on board systems. Marie-Claire's tactical officer tracked them for several seconds and then coolly confirmed *Both targets destroyed captain.*

Good! she declared publicly, though she was not going to reward Vasos by complimenting him on the outcome of his indiscipline *Getting too smart this one. He'll want promotion soon*, she muttered to herself.

Las Palmas

08.33 UTC April 3rd

ZR23D184 had been the poorest item Adams had assembled in preparation for his plan. Not that this said a great deal. Driven by his religious zeal –or rather blinded by his religious zeal- Adams was often oblivious to vices and avarice in others. An apparent, profound conformity to the faith was enough to allay any doubts he might have about the honesty of others, and so it was that those who had been charged with acquiring the munitions and components required for his mission had achieved considerable variations in quality during their acquisitions. Not that this was always their fault.

Timer mechanisms, to take a simple example, ranged from military quality such as those captured from the old Federal facility at Los Alamos to pirated designs such as ZR23D184 made in the Chinese factories which had mushroomed across the globe before the Chinese government had imploded during *The Great Troubles.* On this particular deal, one of the intelligence officers entrusted with the mission had made a personal profit of nearly a hundred gold grams; quality being compromised to personal gain. The same pattern had been repeated in other area, The net result, unknown to Adams, Smith or even Tuckman were an inherent weakness which was about to be revealed.

Even if all had gone according to Adams's master plan, the variations in quality would have frustrated the fine detail demanded by the original. As it was, the initial, premature detonation had already ensured partial failure of his master plan. As the waters disturbed by the original explosion roared back, cascading over the western flank of The Canaries, the remaining mechanisms detonated as scheduled. Not that the nuclear devices which Adams and his men had buried and primed with such precision detonated in exactly the intended sequence, but this was irrelevant given that the intended orientation had already been lost.

These were not large devices. It was not the power but the location which had been central to the plan. In historical terms they would have been classed as tactical warheads, designed to destroy the enemy with a radius of a kilometre or so. The first device, implanted in a fault-line well-known to geologists, had caused a mere three hundred metres or so of the island's western flank to cascade into the sea. Central to Adams's calculations was the explosion's further weakening of the tenuous link between the eastern and western parts of the island. Now – as Adams had initially planned, the chain of explosions deep in the fracture caused the western face of Cumbre Vieja to shear away, but not –as he had planned - like segments of chocolate ice cream scooped from a block with each section folding into the Atlantic in a sequence as the individual, measured charges exploded. Instead, most of the island's western flank, to a depth of a mile or more inland, crashed in a chaotic, tumbling, sliding mass westwards into the Atlantic. In some areas new shorelines and beaches were formed almost immediately, pushing the ocean out but with relatively little impetus. Elsewhere, the land plunged directly and violently into the sea, disappearing into the depths and generating vast waves. In yet other locations the combination of forces was such that the seabed was temporarily laid bare, the debris and force of the impact pushing the water westwards and upwards. To the east, the shockwave hurled across the island, killing all in its path. In about a minute, it arrived on the African coast with sufficient force for the driver of the armoured amphibian in which Adams was seated to believe that they had been hit by a strong gust of wind.

The sequence of explosions in the initial plan had been intended to create a tidal wave of such power that it would destroy the heathen government in Washington and much of what Smith called *..the promiscuous eastern seaboard...* But the sequencing had been crucial, and as the last great slabs of hundreds of millions of tonnes of rock and soil smashed into the Atlantic the impact generated a northerly twist in the mountain of water. Now, rather than heading in an almost directly westerly direction, the face of a water mountain some thousand metres tall shifted substantially and surged northwards.

Eastern end: The Straits of Gibraltar

08.33 UTC April 3rd

Monroe could feel the tremors from the engines of *The Genesis* vibrating in the deck floor. It was an indication of the urgency that the deck commander felt in pushing *Genesis* forward at full speed that he could feel anything at all, for Smith still held him in a vice-like grip, his own body trembling violently with emotion and tears continuing to pour down his face and dripping onto Monroe's left cheek. Looking over Smith's shoulder, Monroe could see Tuckman standing, observing the scene with the mixture of contempt, concern and hatred which Monroe could never fully fathom, but which was increasingly the man's habitual countenance. He had always assumed that the feelings were directed towards himself, but for the first time the thought crossed his mind that Smith might, just might, be its target.

That Smith had not launched into one of his religious tirades or hysterical outbursts was, in itself, a relief for Monroe. His anguish lay in the certainty that 'His' fleet was under attack, a reality reflected both in the engines' vibrations and the irregular bursts of gunfire from the anti-aircraft systems. Despite Smith's hold, he somehow managed to raise his right arm high enough to catch a glimpse of his watch. *'Holy Mother of God!'* he shouted to himself and then mouthed Mr. President. *It is nearly time. Can I please have your permission to return to the deck to ensure that all is going to plan.* As though Monroe's words had suddenly returned him to reality, Smith immediately froze and then pulled himself away, wiping his face on his sleeve as he did so. He looked at his own watch. *Of course Admiral, you should go immediately,* he concluded. *I shall be with you in a matter of minutes to see our endeavours bear fruit. I was simply ...... simply overcome with emotion at our successful transit into the Mediterranean. Into the sea on which St. Paul himself once sailed and our Saviour Jesus Christ indeed may have swum and...*

Mr. President. Brother, Sir. Tuckman interrupted. *Time is passing and the Admiral should either be on the bridge or you should issue orders for him to be relieved.*

Relieved? On what grounds? Monroe demanded, fear returning.

No, no, Smith replied calmly. *There are no grounds for the immediate relief of Admiral Monroe, Brother Tuckman. Please Admiral. Do go ahead to the bridge. We shall be coming up immediately to observe the consequences of God's work.* He extended his hand to Monroe and then wrapped his second hand around Monroe's as the admiral took his. *Go in God's peace now,* and he almost propelled Monroe away. Monroe turned swiftly and almost ran out of the cabin towards the bridge. However, '*No grounds for the immediate relief of Admiral Monroe.*' was not something which had escaped him. '*What are those two planning next?*' he demanded of himself as he sprinted up to the next deck level. Then, as an after -thought, he modified his rhetorical question to '*What is Tuckman planning next for the two of us?*'

Altitude thirty one thousand metres.
Twenty nine kilometres west of Cadiz wastes
08.37 UTC April 3rd

It was the distant horizon radar systems on the intelligence dirigibles which first detected the Atlantic mountain ocean moving up from the south. Detected rather than identified was the correct term, for having analysed established parameters, and having failed to identify the nature of the phenomenon, the computers returned the problem to a human.

The human faced with this particular dilemma, a young lieutenant from the Croatian province, scratched his head and gave the problem back to the computers whilst making a mental note that the software was well over-due a major service. So time passed.

The strategy room on La Cité du Québec was the next to notice something was amiss, but the senior officers had been re-allocated responsibilities with the tactical warfare team, leaving a chief petty officer second class from Montreal in command. Though not her role, her mind was primarily focused on the monitors showing Christian aircraft still attempting to penetrate the ship's defences. Again, the computer systems on La Cité could not identify the nature of the phenomenon and reported a potential fault to the human- who then requested a fault self-assessment from the computers. So time passed.

On the N1 30 miles north east of Tarfaya
08.41 UTC April 3rd

Adams had decided that they were now high enough to permit a halt and view the results of his years of planning. He had made the point of bringing the most powerful pair of binoculars he could find in the ships' stores with him and from this slightly raised elevation on the N1 he calculated that he should have a good view of the Atlantic, and would be able to observe the effects of his explosions. According to all the calculations he and his team had made in there modelling, there should be a visible disturbance on the ocean's surface as the water was pushed in a westerly direction towards the WUCCIES on the eastern seaboard. According to the models, several hours later, having destroyed the enemy on the western coast, there would be a return of the water creating a relatively small tsunami on the west African and European coasts. This was of no importance. It would kill only Unbelievers, for by that time the Christian fleet would be safe in the sheltered waters of the Mediterranean and he and his men would be several hundred miles to the north east in the foothills of the Atlas Mountains.

He peered through the glasses, took them from his eyes, rubbed them to clear the smear on the lenses but could still not see the expected glistening of the sea in the distance. He looked again at his watch. *Another thirteen minutes rest men!* he shouted without thinking, and plucking the figure meaninglessly. The comment was intended for the benefit of those within hearing range, but as no one within hearing range was privy to the details of the plan, he provoked only a raising of puzzled faces. *Thirteen? Unlucky number, better wait a bit before saying anything else*, he mumbled to himself before climbing onto the amphibian to gain some extra height. Standing on the gearbox casing gained him a good two metres from the road surface, though he found himself swaying uncertainly on the slippery surface.

Once again he put the binoculars to his eyes, and fiddled with the focus. *Should have tried these before today*, he found himself muttering several times. He stopped, making a mental note to avoid further muttering – a sure sign of the strain he had been under but a habit which would rapidly lose him authority amongst his troops. Finally, he managed to focus the lenses correctly on the far distance where rain clouds still came down to the horizon to meet the sea. Suddenly, his jaw dropped with shock as he realised that there were no clouds stretching down to the sea, but the sea which was stretching up to the cloud-laden heavens. '*This should not be happening already*,' was his first thought, and then he realised with horror that, rather than racing westwards as he had planned, the waters were tearing in a more northerly direction. Pushed by the sheer volume and force of the main wave, lesser waves were piling onto the coast and, like the parting of the Red Sea for Moses, the water was now driving towards his current location, threatening to engulf his men as it had done the Egyptians thousands of years earlier. *Five seconds to get back on board! All of you, now!! Driver, maximum speed on my command!!* he screamed, blank faces looking up at him in astonishment.

God protect us! Lord God, we have done your work!! he found himself shouting as he jumped down and scrambled into the vehicle. Without waiting for the last men to climb back in, he screamed an order to start moving. The man hesitated long enough for Adams to reach for his sidearm – enough for two more to tumble in. Realising the significance of Adams's move, the driver decided that life was a preferential option, crashed into gear, and lurched forward with his foot flat on the accelerator disregarding the cries of those left behind. As he did so, Adams glanced in horror at his watch. '*Is the time wrong? Have the Europeans prematurely detonated one of the bombs?*' he demanded of himself, and then, as the enormity of what was happening fully hit him, he asked himself the key question: *Has the fleet reached safety*?

Chapter XII
Best Laid Plans
Altitude six thousand metres.
Twenty seven kilometres south east of Cadiz wastes
08.39 UTC April 3rd

Henry had finally been persuaded to waddle back to his seat. Amidst much mirth, Marie-Claire had opened his communications channel, and was explaining the intricacies of dealing with body functions whilst wearing a flight suit. She was less than happy at losing a gunner from his post, but there was no immediate threat from the Americans who had suddenly abandoned formation and were streaming eastwards in an undisciplined route to the protection offered by their fleet's air defence potential. The Christian forces had sustained surprisingly high casualties, and once again Marie-Claire had a sense of unease. '*Could it be'* she asked herself '*the Americans use these ships and aircraft as expendable elements in a larger game? To what end? Or the American commander simply under-estimated our capacity?'* Suddenly, the Canadian was back in her head, repeating the demand for information which he had been anxiously waiting for. *Sorry captain,* was all she could say. *About the thing to the south, I'm still waiting for clarite - for clarification from my Intelligence. But you could turn back east now. The Christians are running away. If your damage is ok you could have fun with them. And we could help you with fuel and repairs. No?* She lacked the authority to speak a word of what she had just uttered, but she could not believe for a second that Central Command would fail to support her –the Canadians would be welcome, if only because their arrival would enable Intelligence to crawl over the vessel in the most detailed but genteel of manners . No one could have missed how ably La Cité had dealt with both Christian aircraft and surface vessels. To the best of her knowledge, the European Federal Navy had no vessels of the same class and, having seen the size of the Christian armada, she was convinced that without external help they would be able to dominate the Mediterranean.

There was what she took to be an angry silence from La Cité, and she took the opportunity to quickly re-check her sensors. The fire on the vessel had been extinguished rapidly, leaving what appeared to be relatively limited damage. Without doubt there would have been casualties, but a first analysis bore testimony to the quality of Canadian construction - Lagard continued to have command of a formidable fighting unit. Suddenly, it occurred to her that she had planned to do her own, deeper, scan of the American vessels, but had forgotten this amidst the other pressures..

Namur, a full, detailed on those two enemy ships, not the Canadian, the ones which is drifting, as soon as possible, she barked, handing this task to the officer who had just eased his way into the co-pilot's seat. He was a middle-aged sous-lieutenant who, appropriately originated from the hills near the new Belgium coastal belt. He bristled visibly at the atypical abruptness of her command and replied simply with a curt *As commanded.*

Shit, merde, not a good way to manage my crew, she reflected briefly before a further wave of complaints from the crews stuck in the defence aircraft came through. There were clearly now no immediate threat to justify a launch and the crews were justifiably complaining about the cold. She could, she felt, almost sense the relief across her squadron following her order to disembark from the fighters, her own pilot being helped out with the help of a gunner and swearing savagely in a range of languages which Marie-Claire could not always follow but seemed to focus on the stupidity of her contradictory orders. *Things may change in a few minutes, but you will perhaps fight – and die?- better if you are at least warm,* she reflected, deliberately disregarding the insults.

38 miles north east of Tarfaya
08.41 UTC April 4th

The road had finally started to climb and turn inland. Adams kept looking backwards. The wall of water which had once been in the distance as a greyish-blue wall was now a towering mass which roared along the coast and swept inland whenever the contours gave it the slightest encouragement. The amphibian lurched and jumped along the road like a deranged kangaroo. No longer driven by Adams's hysteria, his driver had fully appreciated the danger soon after their last stop, alerted by shouts from troopers in the back of the vehicles who had spotted the advancing waters and were now torn between staying low in the vehicle to avoid being thrown out at the next bend of bump, or glancing in fixed horror as it rapidly gained on them. *Faster!* he shouted again at the driver.

As fast as it will go!! the man replied above the roar of the engine, all respect for authority gone. Suddenly, rounding a bend they encountered a section of road which had clearly been recently repaired. The treads gained grip, pushing the vehicle forward, and in the distance Adams saw the rise leading to the plateau which he prayed to God would lift them clear of the pursuing water. He looked back again. *If God is with us we will be saved!* he shouted and then realised that by using the *'If'* word he had publicly committed heresy.

Altitude thirty one thousand metres.
Twenty nine kilometres west of Cadiz wastes
08.43 UTC April 3rd

The Military Intelligence Service computers aboard the dirigibles were still busy working, attempting to analyse something which they had not been programmed to analyze, and busy suggesting that they should be stood down for a fault check, when a technician on the most westerly European dirigible finally recognised the significance of the image on the radar. The reason was purely chance - she was old enough to have been on duty on a cruise ship in the Pacific many years earlier when the vessel had encountered a relatively small tsunami.

The image was not one she would ever forget, and once the source had been identified it was a simple matter to re-programme the computers to analyse the evolving profiles of the waves and so to compute both the speed and direction of the waves. The traumas inflicted on the Atlantic by the disappearance of much of Las Palma had generated two mountainous surges. The main part was speeding roughly in a northerly-westerly direction at some five hundred miles per hour, but the double explosions had incidentally generated a second, smaller wave which the radar showed was cresting along the North African coast and gaining height when constricted by the shore as it approached the old town of Agadir. A few basic calculations indicated that the water would pose no threat to any of the dirigible squadrons or aircraft at their current height, but some further modelling showed that the coasts of the Spanish and Portuguese provinces, and the Walls at Cadiz and Lisbon amongst others, lay directly in its path. What would happen further north and west was still being calculated by the software. *Captain, quickly, look at this!* she shouted to her commander *Quickly sir! This is a disaster!*

Altitude six thousand metres.

Twenty seven kilometres south east of Cadiz wastes

08.46 UTC April 3rd

Marie-Claire knew the commander of their Intelligence support section well. She had slept with him once before he had decided to marry and have a child – something she could still not bear to do herself – and had since met the wife and little girl. They had a small house on a hillside just outside PortoWall so she immediately identified the immense tension in his voice as he broadcast the first warning across the entire military communications network. Warnings were already being relayed as speedily as possible along the entire western coast of the Confederation. She could only imagine the immediate terror which would be ensuing as the flood sirens would – mysteriously – be breaking into the morning's work. As always, there would be that percentage -which seemed to increase every year- which would simply disregard the warning and stay outside the local Wall. Then there would be another percentage whose conscience would be pricked by their historical opposition to spending more on Wall defences or had even failed to do their WallWork and then…

Her calculation stopped in mid-flow as she suddenly remembered the Canadian warship. Whether they had been monitoring the appropriate frequency and just the right time would be a matter of chance, and the probability lay in their still awaiting a response from her. *And that was when?* she demanded of herself and realized to her horror that nearly a quarter of an hour had passed. Without a second's thought, or permission from her superiors, she opened a channel to La Cité.

Lagard had turned ashen by the time Marie-Claire had summarised the situation for him. He paused momentarily, desperately -and fruitlessly- seeking an alternative strategy, before turning to the young ensign at the helm. *Full speed back into The Straits. Execute immediately!* he snapped, the atypical abruptness in his voice immediately communicating the urgency of the situation. There was nothing else he could do. The ship was already at battle station, bulwarks had been closed to minimise the threat from fires or a hull breach, and amidst incredulous glances from the crew he ordered that survival suits be prepared as an eventuality. '*Should I order the removal of body armour?*' he demanded of himself '*That would give them more chance of surviving if she sinks? No,*' he concluded, '*our only chance of survival lies in making it deeply into The Straits before the ship is crushed like a child's toy. It's proved to be a great ship, and I'd love to see some American faces when we pop through The Straits. The armour will be needed when we meet the crazies on the other side,*' though at the back of his mind convictions reappeared that this had probably been a suicide mission from the time they had received their first orders. '*A ship and its crew sacrificed for diplomatic purposes. Not original!*' was the closing thought as he was disturbed by the latest up-date on the damage his ship had already sustained.

Western Mediterranean
08.47 UTC April 3rd

It was not until he had reached the bridge that Monroe realised what a mess Smith had made of his uniform whites. His shoulders were soaked with what he took to be tears and a green slime whose provenance he did not wish to guess. After a few seconds a crewman hesitatingly gestured to Monroe, proffering a suit of body armour from one of the lockers. He was unsure whether the offer was for cosmetic or practical reasons, but a large plume of water near the bow of one of the forward destroyers swayed Monroe in favour of the latter and abruptly brought him back to the reality that they were still under attack. He hastily grabbed the jacket, thanking the man for his kindness. He quickly glanced at the console displaying the status of fleet while putting on the armour. To his surprise, his order for a detailed assessment from the tactical warfare team provoked an instant protestation that the conflict was continuing and the data unreliable. He was probably one of Tuckman's men but he was instantaneously silenced by another voice Monroe recognised as belonging to one of his own.

The damage was relative. Despite the best efforts of his ship's defences and the limited air cover, the damage the Europeans had been able to inflict was evident in the form of simple, florescent crosses on the screen. Given the sheer size of the armada, the loss of a few ships counted for little, though Monroe was dismayed to see that two large soul carriers had been sunk – a loss of over six thousand Christian brothers and sisters on two vessels alone. Another of his destroyers had also been sunk, considerable damage inflicted on a range of other ships, and the air cover had been virtually obliterated with only minimal damage inflicted on the enemy. This development was profoundly disturbing. True, he had launched only older aircraft, but these same models had been capable of easily destroying the European air force during the last conflict. He had not expected this loss of aircraft and crews, though without the air cover his ships would have been easy targets for even a novice flyer in the narrow confines of The Straits. So, it was undeniable that the aircraft had been vital in keeping the Europeans occupied.

Now, with every passing minute his ships were able to take advantage of the greater maneuverability provided by the growing gulf between the Spanish and North African shores. True, it was still dangerous to venture close to the coast , and to Monroe's surprise the odd short-range

missile was still being fired from Moslem positions on the North African side, but the fortifications at Gibraltar had been largely silenced and were to the rear of many of his ships. Ahead, the European naval forces detected so far were such that they would be swiped aside with little effort, but the massed air attacks were starting to impact on his command and could not be disregarded. *Poor leadership this!* he concluded to everyone within hearing. *They shouldn't have delayed, but launched a combined attack rather than leaving their forces divided in this way. It will cost them dearly.*

His growing sense of confidence was suddenly shattered when the horrifying possibility dawned that, without any aerial opposition, the Europeans might decide to sink the vessels he had left in The Straits. True, they appeared to be no more than floating, burning hulks – that was how they had been designed- but if they were sunk for idle target practice, or if the Europeans decided to investigate them more fully, then the entire second part of the plan would be lost and lives have been lost for nothing. With the skies now almost totally in enemy hands, the only way of continuing to distract the enemy would be to launch more aircraft -his first line craft this time. Alternatively, what was starting to be a dangerously delayed Stage Two could be implemented. With God's Will, it could be assumed that during this event large numbers of enemy aircraft and dirigibles would be damaged or destroyed, but as always between Monroe and God loomed Smith - and increasingly Tuckman.

Coincidental with this thought, he sensed a change in the bridge which warned him that the two had arrived. He had no need to turn his head. On *The Genesis,* and almost universally across the fleet if Monroe's informants were correct, the stresses of the past days had fragmented the armada into parties supportive of either Smith or himself. Failure to support The President was both heretical and treasonous, and if the reaction of the bridge crew was a guide, Monroe was drifting into a situation in which he could be deemed to be the leader of an anti-Presidential faction.

Monroe looked at the bridge chronometer again; looking at time pieces had become a nervous habit. Smith had been insistent that 08.33 was a religiously apposite time and that stage two of their plans would be implemented simultaneously with the detonation of the devices planted in Las Palmas, but there had been no confirmation from Adams that all had gone well. The last reports had simply confirmed that all the explosives had been planted and timed and that Adams had landed on the Moroccan coast. According to the original calculations, they had until roughly 09.20 before the effect of the first explosion would be apparent at the western end of The Straits. Stage Two would have to be implemented by then to ensure that the two blockade vessels were not carried off station. However, Monroe's sudden realisation of the vulnerability of their project required more urgent action and his need now was to ensure that Smith acted – and acted with considerable haste.

Mr President, Christian Brother, a word Sir if I may, he called across the bridge. He immediately regretted his words. There was no breach of etiquette as such, but Smith's face showed immediate displeasure. It was combination which was increasingly difficult to find- and which would trigger a positive response. Smith looked across at him, his emotional turmoil of only a few minutes earlier having seemingly vanished, before muttering something to Tuckman. He glanced across at Monroe with his customary hostility before gesturing him over. *Another problem admiral?* Tuckman demanded as soon as Monroe had joined them.

Not a problem Mr. President, Monroe replied instantly, addressing Smith himself and deliberately avoiding Tuckman's *stare but a need to act immediately on the second stage of our plan.*

Already admiral? Is the entire fleet safely deployed? Tuckman demanded without leaving Smith the opportunity to reply.

Mr President, Monroe continued, again deliberately disregarding Tuckman's intervention *if the enemy now chooses to investigate closely we may lose the opportunity to activate our devices. We must launch more aircraft in sufficient numbers to fully engage the Europeans or detonate our bombs immediately. I would suggest..*
And what happened to our earlier aircraft admiral? Was their use badly planned? Were out losses in vain? Tuckman demanded. *And you haven't answered my question – is the entire fleet safely through The Straits and out of danger?*
Monroe blanched. He had lost count of the number of times Tuckman had over-ridden the president's status in recent days, and had been astonished that Smith had allowed his blatant disrespect for rank and growing arrogance to go unchallenged. Clearly The President was under a huge amount of stress, as were they all, but even within recent weeks Monroe had seen individuals executed for far less. But to be challenged here, on the bridge of his own flagship here, and in front of his own crew? Suddenly, and to his own surprise, Monroe felt a flood of anger replace his fear.
I was talking to The President, not to you Tuckman. Unless you are now president of the Christian Confederation? In his anger he had spoken so loudly that all heads on the deck turned. He had not planned it, but his final words were unwittingly the most devastating he

could have uttered. There was an immediate cessation of conversation, contrasting vividly with the background chatter of anti-aircraft fire. For once, it was Tuckman who paled. He looked around quickly. Apart from two marines from the Presidential Guard, the deck was dominated by Monroe's crew -who could be counted upon to support their admiral.

Admiral Monroe is perfectly correct, Mr. Tuckman Smith replied with unusual alacrity. *He is the professional in charge here – entrusted by myself and The Grand Council. Would you wish to challenge this?* he demanded with an evident determination which had been missing in recent days. Tuckman paled further, fearful of the corner he was talking himself into.

No Mr. President but... he started, but was immediately silenced. *No 'buts' now Mr Tuckman. Admiral, your best advice if you please*, Smith barked. *And may I suggest the crew focuses on its business* he added to further drive home his authority. The bridge crews had been watching the drama unfold, bust such was Smith's reputation for harsh discipline that his words had an instantaneous affect, and without exception they resumed their duties.

Monroe looked again at the main battle console. Fresh waves of European aircraft could be seen forming up to the north west and another group was swarming around the pitiful remnants of his own aircraft as they desperately attempted to escape. Behind these, and further to the north and west, several groups of enemy dirigibles were poised, the scanners revealing that they were still loaded with their protective fighters.

He hesitated, aware of the crucial importance of the next few words. *My best advice Christian Brother President,* Monroe finally announced slowly, weighing the importance of each word, *is that we wait a few more minutes, enough time to warn all our ships to batten down, and then we go to Stage Two. We may lose a few ships, but if we lose those these,* and he jabbed his finger on the screen where two red dots were fixed at the narrowest point of The Straits *who knows what may come hunting us in due course. In the future, this sea could become either ours to control, or a bottleneck into which any enemy may venture. You will recall Mr. President, the brilliance and simplicity of the original plan. We can make this God's sea again if we act swiftly. The Mare Nostrum as it was in the time of Our Lord Christ.* Smith hesitated and then looked directly out of the bridge. In the distance, too far to be able to identify its loyalties, an aircraft was spinning in flames towards the ocean. He blinked convulsively at the sight, almost as though taken aback by this display of violence so close to himself, but not within his control. Turning back to Monroe, his eyes steadied. *What time do you have admiral?* he asked softly.

08.52 Mr. President. Monroe replied.

An untidy time. Not one that smacks of history don't you agree Mr. Tuckman? Tuckman looked up. For the past few seconds his head had been down, like a scolded child or someone caught in the commission of some sin. Now he raised his head, puffed up his chest as though he felt a new, warm, wave of approval and replied clearly *I agree fully Christian Brother President. Should you not establish a proper time and inform the fleet so that they will have the honour of seeing your plan, and that of Our Lord God, further develop?* It was a brilliantly crafted sentence which appealed simultaneously to Smith's ego and religious beliefs.

A superb proposal, Smith replied emphatically, cutting short the protest which was forming on Monroe's lips. *Let me see now, 08.33 we have missed, so let us go for 09.13 – holy minutes representing our Lord and his disciples seems significant enough and we can abandon the old nonsense. We can do away with the old myth about unlucky 13 can we not? Please to arrange events accordingly admiral - and I shall address the fleet on a secure link from my state room.*

Eighteen kilometres south west of Cadiz wastes.

Altitude sixteen thousand five hundred metres.

08.55 UTC April 4th

It was a young, Polish caporal chef serving as co-pilot on the lead intelligence dirigible who first detected it. '*It*', was an unpredicted and unseen consequence of the oceanic convulsions whose after-shock was hurtling forward many miles to the south and thousands of metres below them, but '*it*' was a surge of air forced forward and upwards by the mountainous waters racing northwards. The pressure exerted would have been relatively insignificant for fixed-wing aircraft, but the dirigibles, and especially the large intelligence units with their radar domes and other external encumbrances, were fragile sensitive affairs. Consequently, the pressure exerted by the front of the shock wave was enough to nudge the dirigible gently but incessantly to port, and then the constant pressure served to drive the craft further to the north and east and higher and higher into the skies. For several seconds her reaction was to suspect a systems malfunction on her own craft, but then the communications bands filled with alarmed calls, shouts, orders and counter-commands from crafts. Then, their commander's voice cut through the cacophony, ordering the pilots to maintain their distance but to allow the air currents to carry them northwards. She checked the altimeter and turned to her pilot. *What are the weather conditions here at the higher altitude!* she demanded and pointed at the altimeter which had already passed the seventeen thousand mark and was climbing rapidly.

Don't know, but they are going to be smashed if they stay there, he retorted, and gesticulated at the display console whose blinking green dots revealed the squadron of attack dirigibles far below them to the south east. *Have they been warned?*

Altitude six thousand two hundred metres.

Twenty three kilometres south east of Cadiz wastes

08. 57 UTC April 3rd

The priority call from Intelligence was an additional, unwanted demand. Marie-Claire's communication channels were already awash with questions from commanders whose on board systems were alerting them to sudden, unplanned changes in altitude and position. Worse, part of the value of the call from Intelligence was lost as the hyper- excited operator jumped intermittently between languages – the English and German elements she could follow, but there were some additional words whose provenance she could guess but whose meaning was lost. Overall, it was simple, abrupt, lacking in details and leaving her only with the knowledge that, for some reason, turbulence from the south was

impacting on all of the western squadrons and she was ordered to immediately increase height and disperse her command.
She immediately recognized the dangers in this, given that there was still a risk of another attack. The greater the gaps between the dirigibles the less able they were to provide mutually supportive fire. However, the sudden changes in air currents were increasing the risk of collisions and she had vivid memories of such an occurrence from her days as a trainee pilot. The event had deeply shocked her, not least because of the rapidity with which the crafts had lost stability -despite being divided into, theoretically, autonomous chambers. If punctured deeply enough there was always the risk of cabling being severed and it was assumed that such a combination of electrical sparks and flammable gases had proved fatal in the incident she had witnessed. The sight of the crumpled envelope plummeting to the earth in flames with her comrades on board was deeply embedded in her memory.
A further complication lay with many of the dirigibles still carrying single, armed aircraft. The dirigibles could cope with all but the most extreme turbulence when fully laden and with the fighter screen. Though carefully stowed, carrying only one

aircraft was not optimum for stability. If the turbulence increased, she would have to consider ordering the fighters launched, leaving her command unprotected when the aircrafts' fuel was exhausted.

She was struggling with ramifications of these issues when Namur suddenly shot from his seat at one of the consoles and lumbered towards her at a speed she had never previously seen in a flight suit. She had forgotten that she had given him the task of scanning the American vessels and was about to request a new rendezvous point from him when he thrust a detachable monitor in his hand *Look!* he shouted, unnecessarily, given their proximity. *Look what the detailed analysis has shown. This is a trap!* Marie-Claire grabbed the monitor clumsily with her large flight gloves. The Straits and the two ships in it were clearly visible, the two American vessels distinguished by the intensity of an orange glow amid ship. La Cité du Québec was also visible, just re-entering the western end of The Straits at great speed.

So? she demanded. *They are on fire. I knew that, what is so urgent? What is this thing about a trap?* she demanded brusquely.

Capitaine! Namur almost deafened her with his shouting. *Here is the radiation spectrum,* and he adjusted the monitor to reveal another colour. *Those two ships look like they are on fire, but it is all not true - artificial. They want to look like a fire, but they are floating bombe nucleaire! If they explode they will destroy everything for kilometres, including us.*

Marie-Claire hesitated, unwilling to accept the truth of the data before her eyes. *You are sure?* though in her heart she already knew that this explained all her misgivings.

I am sure it is a ship filled with uranium and plutonium, Namur replied instantly.' The way she is made, the fire – not a real fire - of this I am certain. It looks like a bomb. What the Americans plan... this I do not know. But this is a trap for someone.

Within minutes the pilots were once again scrambled into their cockpits, launched immediately and flew away northwards at full speed.. As soon as they had cleared, the dirigibles also swung northwards, engines working at maximum power to increase distance and gases pumped into the skin to increase height. The turbulence from the south and west now proved an asset in giving an additional boost to speed and altitude.

As they climbed, Marie-Claire broadcast a stream of encrypted warnings to the Intelligence vessels to her west and the European aircraft now reforming to attack the American fleet itself.

Chapter XIII
Consequences
09.00 UTC April 3rd

Despite their profound and repeated prayers for a successful mission, neither Smith nor Adams had successfully communicated the importance of punctual chronology to the Atlantic Ocean. Not that the Ocean itself could be blamed for its failure to cooperate fully. It was itself, as already noted, the innocent victim of some shoddy workmanship and corrupt business dealings which had already modified the plans Adams had so carefully developed. At this very moment Adams himself was lying in the desert scrub. God had at least heard his prayers to the extent of saving his life, and those of some of his command. The lead three vehicles – he had immediately concluded that the symbolism of the holy trinity was inherent in this – had managed to out-run the water. Just. The final force of the water had broken over them, but with its energy mostly exhausted it had served no more than to push the vehicles off the road rolling and into a shallow depression, leaving any surviving occupants floundering in their newly acquired swimming pools. The rear vehicles had gone, perhaps carried into some gorge or buried in the sand and other detritus which had been dumped to form a new hillock. Even as he himself struggled into an upright position, Adams saw the soil on the hillock convulse and a head emerge- evidence that another of his men had survived thanks to God's benevolence.

Altitude seven thousand three hundred metres. Twenty kilometres south east of Cadiz wastes 09.00 UTC April 3rd

Henry had found the entire experience thus far so uncomfortably tiresome that he had been sleeping huddled up against a life raft. Out of pity, one of the gunners had located it for him and wedged it against a pair of converging ribs forming the framework over which the dirigible's skinned stretched. Henry's childhood-formed expectations had been of greater action- certainly the sight and sound of chattering guns, hissing missile engines and enemy aircraft and vessels sent to their doom. Without risk to himself of course. There was even a small part of his vanity which hoped that he would suddenly be called upon to explain the mysteries of Smith's strategy, though the more honest part of him knew that he had long since abandoned any pretext to understanding what was happening. An attack on The Canaries had never featured in any of his night-long discussions with Smith.

Drifting into sleep had been much more pleasurable, though his dreams were perplexing with both Rachael and Marie-Claire drifting in and out in what became increasingly erotic encounters. But now things had changed and he found himself yearning for the security of only seconds earlier. He shot from his sleep to the sound of alarms and shouts and clangs and hissing gases which, he assumed, were associated with a distinct feeling of his stomach being left behind. Looking through the portal, he could see other dirigibles breaking formation and, judging from the morning sun, moving rapidly in a northerly direction.
What's happening!? he shouted into his mouth piece. There was no reply, but a swift glance at the dirigible's crew immediately revealed a new tension. For some reason the portholes were being closed, blocking out the welcome rays of the morning sun, and without warning a gloved hand shot past his face, pulling his own closed. He twisted backwards in his seat, irritated both by being disturbed and his ignorance of events. *What are you doing that for?* he demanded, unsure even if the words carried beyond the resonating confines of his helmet. There was a silence, then the sound of a struggle for the right word.

Flash! Danger for eyes! eventually communicated brusquely, leaving Henry none the wiser. The turning back communicated an end to the conversation. Feeling less than enlightened by '*Flash! Danger for eyes!'* He was tempted to stumble his way to the command section and demand an explanation from Marie-Claire when an enormous lurch reminded him of the fragility of both the craft and of his own stomach. He settled back in his seat. '*Flash! Danger for eyes! What kind of gibberish is that?*' he mused to himself, and found himself thinking impolite things about the quality of Europeans English. *Should have stayed with American and not gone for German and French*, he muttered, secure that no one was listening.

Shut up! immediately proved him wrong It was Marie- Claire's voice but it carried a novel tension and an assertiveness.

I just wanted to know what is happening and..

I said shut up! You ave no value now and some would be appy to drop you out. So silence! We are in danger!

Even though he could not see through the face visors the tension was almost palpable as Henry looked around the confines of the craft. The machine guns had been stowed back in their racks and the gun ports closed, so it was evident that there was no immediate expectation of any enemy attack.

Don't know what is going on here but The French bitch has clearly had a bad flight. I sometimes do wonder who the real enemy is here. he mumbled to himself, ensuring the microphone speaker was off. He had had to check himself on the use of the word *enemy* of course– there were, after all, thousands of American military personal around London and elsewhere in the country – but his instincts told him that they were not the crazy Christian lot in which he had now classified Smith's party. *When the hell is this charade going to end and I can go home?* was the final question as he drifted back to sleep.

The Straits of Gibraltar

09.04 UTC April 3rd

La Cité du Québec was ploughing through the waters of The Straits with all the power her engines could muster and with her multiple hulls trimmed to minimise drag. Ahead, off his port bow, Lagard could just see the smoke rising from one of the Christian ships which he now realised had been slowly sailed north in The Straits and was now less than a mile off shore. The other ship was not within sight, but his electronics confirmed that a plume - of what he now understood to be artificial smoke – revealed its position close to the southern shore. Despite his attempts to maintain his usually controlled demeanour, the tension on his face was evident to the entire command deck. It was not enough to be attempting to outrun the mountainous seas that the Americans had already unleashed, but the garbled message from the Europeans had warned him that he was fleeing directly into a nuclear device scheduled to explode at some unknown time – but when?

Suddenly, the Christians' intention hit him. *God, you know what those bastards are going to try and do?'* he blurted out to no one is particular, though more than a dozen heads turned. *I'll bet my pay for the year they are going to try and block The Straits! That will be the best way they can protect themselves from the Federal navy.* The horrendous, inevitable logic of his position came home. To try and escape the ocean devastation the Americans had unleashed, he had no choice but to bring his vessel past this threat. Military logic decreed that he should seize the opportunity, destroying the vessels as he passed them. Hopefully, the conventional explosions would destroy or disable the nuclear explosives or place them at the bottom of the sea where their impact would be minimised. If he failed? Well, the consequence would be no worse than having failed to act.

Armaments, prepare four missile salvos! he snapped into his radio. *Tactical command, range on the two hostile targets notified by our European friends.*

Western Mediterranean

09.05 UTC April 3rd

As soon as *My Dearest Christian Brothers and Sisters...* eased from Smith's lips, Monroe knew that this would be one of the longer speeches and the detonation deadline would probably have to be changed. Smith had a limited range of formats which he used to introduce his public addresses. *Fellow Christians* usually lasted less than a couple of minutes, *Beloved Christians* a good five. *My Dearest,* followed by a number of possible combinations, about ten. Thankfully, he had not entered into *Beloved Fellow Souls* which inevitably involved some theological discourse and rarely lasted less than an hour. In the early years Smith had been a brilliant orator, one of the reasons for his election as President, but recently the quality of his oration had matched his other faculties in being increasingly unreliable in quality and lacking any inspirational value. Something had happened to the man; Monroe suspected Tuckman's involvement, but how and why?

As Smith's voice continued to drone from the speakers, Monroe took the opportunity to look around the command deck. There was a cross-section of ranks and ages and he knew both the names and loyalties of almost every individual. There were a couple of senior officers who had been with him from the earliest days of the Christian navy and were totally loyal. At the other extreme were a couple of new marine guards whom Tuckman had insisted be assigned for *additional security* and were doubtless immediate conduits of any title tattle directly to their master.

Then there was the ensign manning one of the battle consoles and gesticulating to him wildly. Monroe shook his head as though to dispel the image and then, grateful for the opportunity to do something more interesting than listen to Smith, he strode over to the man's post. Convention had it that all but the most important duties should be abandoned when Smith was delivering one of his.... What was it? A lecture? A sermon? A mixture of the two? Monroe had never been fully able to decide, but his was immediately aware that his apparent lack of respect caused every eye on the deck to swivel and follow him. Turning a head might have been too dangerous, too lacking in respect for the President's words, but those who could do dared to follow Monroe until he was standing, towering over the ensign. *Yes?* he demanded. And then, realising that his had communicated an unintended hostility, his tone softened. *What is it ensign...?*

Sir. Sorry to disturb you Sir when the Brother President is addressing us all, but I really do think you should have a look at this. Uncomprehendingly, Monroe glanced at the screen which revealed the European aircraft and dirigibles peeling away rapidly to various points in the north. His initial, brief reaction was one of relief that his ships had been saved another wave of attacks before the implications hit him. '*Holy God. They must have identified our special gift.*' he almost shouted to himself, though he immediately consoled himself with the thought that, typical of the Godless Europeans, they had chosen to flee rather than risk attacking his ships. '*Not much they can do now anyway,*' he concluded, making a rough calculation of the distance between the aircraft and his vessels. '*It's what? 09.07*' he confirmed to himself looking at both the bridge chronometer and his own watch. '*Even if they launched a now missile it would be too...* .' but the thought remained unfinished and he jerked violently upright with the shock of noting a third vessel which he had initially missed.

You wanted to show me this ensign? he demanded, the growing tension evident in his voice. *When did that ship re-enter The Straits? Why wasn't I informed?*

The man licked his lips nervously. *Brother Sir. I was told not to disturb you further.*
By? Monroe demanded, though he already knew the answer before the sailor's lips could twitch again and say *By Christian Brother Tuckman, Sir. Acting on direct orders from The President.*
And you disobeyed the order? Monroe demanded, though his voice had softened and perhaps now communicated some of the gratitude he felt towards the ensign's loyalty to his admiral.
Because I feel you must see this Sir. This is what I wanted you to see, and he ran a pointer along a hazy line on the screen.
You have a fault ensign? Monroe demanded.
No Brother Sir,'the man replied instantly. *The distant sensors indicate what appears to be an enormous wall of water approaching The Straits. The lieutenant* and he pointed to a figure so entranced with Smith's ranting that she was oblivious of Monroe's arrival *has made some calculations and she estimates that part of the water will start to enter The Straits in less than half an hour and …* Another sentence remained unfinished as Monroe noted a further change on the console monitor as La Cité du Québec launched the first of its missiles. He whitened instantly, and to Smith's unrestrained fury, and of shock to all, his voice cut across his benediction as every vessel in the fleet was ordered

to close is bulkheads and he gabbled out the only command he had ever shouted at The President of the Christian Confederation: *Detonate the bombs now for Love of God!*

The Straits of Gibraltar
09.09 UTC

The *Omegas* had taken over a year to construct using the best resources and brains available to the Confederation. The idea was Smith's and, consequently there had been none of the false economies and dodgy dealings which Adams had been forced to engage in. For Smith, the plan fully complemented Adams's own to purge the Wuccies, though his own had the additional benefit of excluding any remaining evil from the New Holy Land.

Both vessels were a masterpiece in terms of nuclear engineering and deception, their nuclear devices being caressed in the centre of a honeycomb of armour, each layer of which was constructed from a different composite to absorb the impact of a different projectile whilst the intervening voids had been carefully engineered to absorb and deflect any resultant blast. Then, to ensure their objective was achieved, the entire structure had been reverse engineered to maximise the potential impact of the explosion generated from within the vessels, and to ensure that the force of the blast was not dissipated on an unwanted vertical axis. Not only did the resulting work provide an almost unequalled level of protection for a floating device, but it was enough to confuse all but the most determined and detailed scanning using radar or the myriad of alternative scanning systems employed by the competing military alliances. Marie-Clair's chance success in identifying the bombs was only thanks to Namur's persistence and originality in trying a variety of scans on a range of spectrums which had finally identified the inevitable, tiny release of radioactive particles. The - not inevitable-result was the explosion on both vessels of two of La Cité's surface-to-surface missiles.

Nova Lisboa

09.09 UTC

Amanda Brown was enjoying her time. The beach on which she lay enjoying the growing warmth of the sun had been skilfully fashioned on the new tidal limits, and incorporated fine, fresh sand which had been excavated by the engineers at the base on the pretext of a training exercise. It was looking like a beautiful morning and she had enjoyed yet another successful night with the locals. *They must be totally dumb. Or too proud or something to talk to each other?* was the dominant theme as she drifted in and out of her dreams. *How is it that they haven't realized that they all wake up with the slightest of headaches?* she questioned, though she struggled to force herself to remember that she had almost exhausted her supply of tiny serum capsules. Was it the type of male, or the climate, or a tribute to her sexual skills? It was not important - but they had all fallen into a deep sleep after having sex with her and it had then been child's play to drop the tiny capsule onto their tongues. Then, they had been truly hers. Whilst she might be considered a bit of a slut for having slept her way through much of the local military, the information divulged under the influence of the drugs would be good for a promotion or two.

She wriggled down further into the towel she had lain on the sand, enjoying the feel as she allowed the sand to slip between her toes. Unusually, there were almost no cries from the local seabirds, though she was vaguely aware of a disturbing drone in the distance. '*Disturbing? Yes, that was the word to describe that dullard Henry. The Europeans were slow-witted enough to have accepted his feeble knowledge of Smith as a basis for his being invited south and she had- naturally – come as his liaison from Foreign Affairs.*' There was another sound now, which was starting to irritate her and disturb her sleep. Playing the great lover and then recording all the information which burbled out as a result of the drug was one thing, but that meant she need to sleep during the day. *'But the dullard Henry never really wanted me. Not good enough…*

The other sound suddenly roared into her reality as the roar of a jeep's engine, the screeching of tyres and brakes and the savage beeping of a horn. She opened her eyes and sat up, looking up the slope towards a dirt track which led down to the beach. The Greek one, Heraklion, was there, and her initial reaction was one of *No, no more sex for now. I've got everything I want from you.* But then she realized that there was a flow of alarmed words from his mouth and a savage gesticulation out to where the ocean seemed to be taking on a new form. Puzzled, she listened more intently and her eyes opened in fear as she finally recognized an almost universal term. *Tsunami!* He was shouting.

15.1 degrees west, 36.0 degrees north
09.09 UTC

Ragler and the crew of the C22 were ruing the day they had, according to official records, saved WashingtonWall from the Christian attack. True, they had enjoyed two promotions in short sequences, but this had been at the expense of their weekend leave and then, with only a minimal of preparation, all three of the latest C crafts had been ordered eastwards to join the Atlantic Fleet far out in the ocean. The journey itself had been a nightmare, encountering the worst weather Ragler had ever flown in. Their landing on the deck of the aircraft carrier USS Reprisal had –as he enjoyed telling all and sundry – as bad as the crash landing after we had encountered the Christian fleet and saved President Lopez. Ragler's opinion of the President, the military and life in general had declined rapidly in a matter of days not least because *I'm an army man and never joined the navy. Hate this. Get sea sick.* and many other terms. Most contained a substantial loading of abusive and potentially seditious vocabulary.

This morning, all three Cs had again been sent forward of the Federal fleet to scan for hostile activity. They had also been told to look for traces of a Federal submarine which seemed to have disappeared without trace, though there was a rumour circulating that it had been seized by Christians or perhaps even destroyed in fighting amongst the crew.

Collins, can you stop humming all the time! he bellowed into his mouthpiece. They had been up for over two hours now and his beloved, heroic navigator/ comms officer, he who had saved The President, had been endangering his own life through incessantly humming the same archaic song from the First Civil War. Something about *John Brown's soul going marching on* was all that seemed to be clear, but it was enough to make Ragler fear that he had converted to the Christians until Collins had explained its link to the first Federal cause. Not that this really made Ragler feel much better, especially as his co-pilot had gone down with field dysentery and he had been lumbered with a navy flyer. A female Pulaski. Not that he had anything against her, but he had just finished training one crew and was not excited at the idea of having to train another out in the open ocean – especially a key member such as the co-pilot.

But on the other hand she was keen and observant though rather excitable as he was just concluding. *What's up?* he demanded, turning his attention from Collins.

Captain, what does this mean? Is this an instrument faulty? she enquired hesitantly. Ragler relaxed momentarily, basking in his new rank before giving the question and attention. *That is....* and he stopped mid-sentence before giving the console a gentle tap as though it was still a mechanical system which could stick. *That must be a fault,* he continued *because that indicates our relationship with the far horizon – very useful for long-distance navigation and ...*

And currently indicating that the horizon is rising while our altitude is static? Polanski concluded enthusiastically. *Exactly, which is rubbish because*...he started before the radio crackled into life. *Captain Ragler, this is Bellingham C21. Can you confirm our altitude and angle according to your radar. We appear have an instrument fault – or do we have an event on our far horizon?*

The Straits of Gibraltar

09.10 UTC

The nuclear devices on the *Omegas* were not detonated as part of a carefully calculated plan full of religious significance, but because neither Christian Confederation President Smith, nor his head of security, had possessed the foresight to incorporate a dual control system into the detonation mechanism. They were also detonated because, in the melee which developed on the bridge of *Genesis,* Monroe had the dual advantages of surprise and size; advantages which were enough for him to wrestle the control from Smith whilst the Presidential brain was still in the middle of a holy sentence and to push the detonation buttons before he was rendered unconscious by a baton from one of the Presidential Guard.

Though engineered to cope with an external attack, the Omegas had also been designed to maximise the directionality of the blast. The bows, which it had been intended should always points shore wards, had been modelled to resist external pressure but to rupture readily when subject to internal pressure allowing the explosive forces generated to burst out. The near-simultaneous detonation of *La Cité's* missiles near the Omegas' vaporizing decks was a further complexity which had not been fed into any equations. So it was that for the second time that day the sea was ripped apart, this time simultaneously on both the northern and southern shores of The Straits.

Despite the quality of their vessel -the best of Canadian engineering design, metals and advanced plastics - the proximity of Laggard and *La Cité* to the combined blasts had instantaneous consequences. Any hope was immediately cancelled of future leave, career, family, making love with beautiful men or women after a night in the bar -life itself. The impact was such that, within a split second it was academic that, rather than the traditional flash followed by a shockwave, there was initially remarkably little visual evidence for the detonations of the five 20 megaton devices stowed on each of the *Omegas*.

Much of the energy, as planned, drove the sea landwards, ripping onshore and dragging back hundreds of millions of tons of rock and soil with it. Following advice for once, Smith had chosen the narrowest part of The Straits, and much of the force of the explosions remained confined within these narrow confines, the enormous waves partly cancelling themselves as they collided whilst sloshing north and south as though rocking in some gigantic trough. Not all of the energy was contained in this way.

The tail of Smith's –or Monroe's depending on the conversation- giant armada was barely clearing Gibraltar when the bombs exploded. Another few minutes of Smith's sermon, and the resultant delay in detonation, would have made some difference as each vessel was now pushing westwards at its maximum speed. As it was, the wave resulting from the force of the detonation and the subsequent landslides was akin to a giant tidal bore containing millions of tons of displaced water out of both ends of The Straits. The resulting wave bore no comparison to that generated by Adams off the Canaries coast, and some of its height and power was lost as it emerged into the wider waters of the Mediterranean, but for some its impact was lethal. In theory, all of the vessels had already battened-down in preparation for the planned detonation, but for some this remained an incomplete process, partly because of the premature nature of the explosion, partly because of the indiscipline or inexperience of some crews and partly because of their distraction in listening to Smith's address. When the Christian President spoke, his world stopped.

Holy Mother of God!' were the words from that same Christian President standing on Genesis's towering bridge. At a distance of over twenty miles, the very crest of the wave was just distinguishable on one of the flight deck monitors located in the rigging, whilst the radar and other systems confirmed the story electronically. For the commander of the rearguard Christian Confederation cruiser *David* the wave represented a towering mass which blotted out the sky, and whose only benefits were that his crew had promptly obeyed orders and this nightmare was at least approaching stern on. *God willing, we shall as least not turn turtle* was his concluding thought as the blast shutters shot into place over the bridge glass.

Mr. Tuckman. Place Admiral Monroe under arrest for .....for dereliction of duty. Smith stammered, barely able to control his fury. *For ...for treason!* he added vehemently for good measure. *Take him away. Get him out of my sight. And then come to my quarters*, he concluded. Tuckman could barely conceal the smile as he ordered two of the Presidential Guards to haul the still unconscious Monroe to his feet and to drag him off to the security pen.

He ruined my speech! Perhaps the best I had ever prepared!

Smith screamed to himself. *And why? How dare he disobey me in that manner. Tuckman, Paul, was right from the beginning. He is no true believer.* With these thoughts he stormed back to his own quarters.

Altitude seven thousand six hundred metres.

Eighteen kilometres south east of Cadiz wastes.

09.10 UTC April 3rd

The Air Force Tribunal ruled that Marie-Claire had been partly responsible for what followed and consequently she was formally reprimanded. If she had remained calmer, and given her squadron clearer instructions, the distance between each dirigible might have been greater when the shock wave from the detonation arrived. On the positive side, as the subsequent military investigation ruled, her crew's collective persistence had saved most of the Southern Command's aircraft from being destroyed. Further, she had saved her own fighters by launching them promptly once the danger had been identified. On the negative side, her entire squadron had been *'...running scared in an uncontrolled and undisciplined manner...'* as the Tribunal termed it. The result was that the dirigibles were still much too tightly bunched when the blast tore into them, tossing the machines wildly like autumn leaves rolling aimlessly in a winter storm.

The first that Henry knew of Marie-Claire's failure in following this fundamental element in her training, was when his peaceful snoozing was shattered by a stream of indecipherable shouts and cries. Under stress, individuals have a strong tendency to revert to their native tongues, and so it was that he could understand the odd word of military-English and some French which filled the gaps between the Spanish, Greek and something else –was the Albanian aboard?- but even without perfect linguistic knowledge it was immediately evident that something was clearly very, very wrong.

As the investigation noted, distance was crucial. The dirigibles closest to the blast were inevitably those which received the greatest impact, forcefully shoving them into nearby crafts. The results were generally lethal. Some of the more distant crafts were relatively unaffected other than experiencing an unwanted roll or two- though this served as a terminal lesson for crew members who had chosen to disregard the importance of using seat restraints. At one level Henry was less fortunate. He had barely finished making a sleep-real-world translation of the French and concluded the thought *This reminds me of Euro Disney as a child. I threw up then* when he opened his eyes in time to witness the dirigible's frame flex violently while simultaneously the entire cylinder was rolled length-wise on its axis. He was left suspended, head-down, his lower torso digging painfully into his straining lap belt. The craft was designed to deal with such eventualities, which were not atypical of extreme turbulence, though if they had still been carrying aircraft these would have been thrust through the thin envelopes of gas on which their lives depended. Without such a cargo, the frame, engines and gas cylinders were sufficiently resilient to simply roll with the impact. However, it was at this point that Henry's already distressed state of mind was further perturbed as another dirigible's propeller blades sliced through the fabric to the rear of his seat. His luck was that there was no inflation gases stored in this particular section and, hence, no immediate explosion. Fortuitously, the impact also provided another partial roll which left him sitting almost upright and cancelled the *I am going to throw up!* sentiment. The bad luck was that the blades continued to rotate, slightly impaired by whatever material was now wrapped round their tips, but with sufficient force to cut through the main horizontal strut on the port side. Critically compromised, the integrity of the whole structure failed.

Fortunately for him, the risk of Henry being turned into some form of minced meat by the motor blades ended at this point, the impact of hitting the strut being sufficient to stall the motor. Then, for a reason perhaps born of the remnants of youthful curiosity, he opened the port hatch in time to see the other craft starting to fall, its fabric rapidly splitting open. *Lucky us!* he concluded, as a stream of what he assumed was aviation fuel spilled from a broken pipe and ignited on the still-hot engine. Marie-Claire had told him that *these things* were built from some form of fire-resistant material, but even so it would only be a matter of seconds before the gas ignited. As though to confirm his thoughts, he saw the first of several bodies drop from the falling craft, the red survival suits highlighted by the morning sky. There was no immediate opening of parachutes but he vaguely remembered that in training the instruction had been to delay opening parachutes to maximise the distance between yourself and a crippled dirigible. After what seemed an interminable delay, four red and white chutes opened- but the other red body he had counted continued its uncontrolled, plummet earthwards.
So how does this chute work again? he demanded of himself with a considerable sense of unease, the sight forcing him to try and remember the training

session they'd had on the first day, and which he had treated with such indifference. *Not something we shall need hopefully, but...* He was about to vocalise his question when he suddenly realised that he was alone in the dirigible apart from a single figure sitting, gesticulating wildly to him, on what had once been the hatch for the aircraft launches. Even in the second or so it took him to realise the implications, he felt a sickening lurch as the nose of the dirigible shifted from a semi-horizontal plane to something he instantly knew was earth-bound.

18.0 degrees west 35.1 degrees north

09.16 UTC April 3rd

If decisions could be un-made, Admiral Joseph Mustafa Kemel Torgut would have un-made his decision to transfer his flag from the *Constitution* to the *John F. Kennedy III.* His initial plan had been to personally supervise the launch of his fighter-bombers when they flew out to attack Smith's forces, and he had taken the opportunity of a relatively calm morning to make the transfer between ships. Now, standing with the messages from his forward scout dirigibles, he deeply regretted the move. The *Kennedy* was a good ship, but he had seen it struggle in the latest storms and had already concluded that this type of super-carrier, huge flat tops with enormous surfaces for the seas to break over, was obsolete - at least in the Atlantic. *Would have been better on the Constitution, she may survive this.* was the sum of his thoughts, though he knew there was still time to save himself by boarding one of the many helicopters and aircraft being scrambled into the potential safety of the skies. As Admiral, he was not prepared to set the example of saving his own life while his command was endangered.

Ragler and Bellingham had provided almost identical calculations as regards the height and speed of the approaching mass, and what could be done was now being done. Communicating with the European coastal defences had proved futile. *Probably in a state of chaos with this coming their way,* he had concluded, but contact with the regional Command in Madrid had proved more productive. Now, anything which could fly was being fuelled to its maximum capacity and stripped of all but the bare essentials to allow passengers to be carried.

With luck, some of them would make it to land and the pilots had been ordered to immediately put themselves at the disposition of the Europeans. He had discussed this urgently with President Lopez and had his full support. *Smith and Monroe may have won this battle, but the war is not finished and they cannot be allowed to win.* was his own dominant thought, though Lopez had put it more bluntly: *Smith's madness will take us back to The Dark Ages. He must be stopped somehow.*

Torgut took out a wallet containing a picture he always carried of his family. He looked at it, and then the crew standing around him on the deck. Each would have their own family and loved-ones and what was the best he could do for them? Captain, I want that order re-broadcast to the entire fleet. *Once aircraft have been launched, I want every bulkhead sealed, every crew member kitted out in their survival gear and every ship closed down as though for a nuclear attack or extreme weather conditions. Is that clear? And.....* he hesitated. No, wait, I shall do that personally. Since the religious wars, the old God Bless America had been largely abandoned, but despite his reservations Torgut had decided to add his own tag to end the repeated order which he broadcast personally on the inter-ship comm: *God Bless America - and Each and Every One of You.*

London Wall Central Travel Hub

09.30 UTC April 3rd

It was that bloody, newly discovered sister of Bart or Henry, or whoever she was married to who disturbed Rachael la Fontaine's sleep. The stupid woman had woken John as well, and then had been so insistent - so insistent that they should come to north. *If Bart, Henry, has warned you to get out of London there will be a good reason!* she had shouted down the phone *So why didn't you take a morning transport as you'd promised!?*

Rachael had finally conceded that her husband was not of an excitable nature and there might be a reason for his demand– though what is was she had no idea. John was also feeling much better and ... when was the last time they had been outside? Indeed, she suddenly realized that John had never been beyond LondonWall and had only once taken a clapped-out commuter train. As soon as she mentioned the idea of visiting some unknown relative he seemed to experience a Lazarus-like revival in his health and was enthused with the idea of what he immediately called *'The Big Journey.'* Rachael herself was both suspicious and intrigued by this newly extended family, and the discovery that Henry had a stash of Travel Credits at the back of his drawer was the clincher.

The booking hall has a gloomy, dirty affair reflecting the reality that those with money or connections didn't generally use public transport. The service reflected this, the queue at the ticket counter being enormous- a mixture of civilians going here and there for whatever reasons, Wall Gangs heading mostly eastwards to the Norfolk Wastes and

military personnel heading for the southern or northern defences. Fortunately, John found the admixture of people intriguing and, a rarity without his Dad or an electronic game being around, he entertained himself despite waiting in line for nearly half an hour. *Names and identity cards,* was the monotonous, repeated demand she could hear from far back in the line, though there was the slightest intake of breath and a shift in the respect gears as the girl who finally served them took her own documents and recognised the rank on the identity card. *Apologies for the wait, a very busy day as you can see. Sorry, but you haven't completed the reason for the journey,* she almost apologized for the extra bureaucracy.
Family visit Rachel' replied after a second's hesitation, and John's head shot up as though to say *'What family?'* though he remained silent.
And date of return? the girl continued, gaining confidence as the potentially-superior one demonstrated neither efficiency nor power. *Can't I leave that blank?* Rachael demanded perplexed. She had last travelled alone before Henry and she had married, and since then Henry or his work had always arranged her travel arrangements.
Yes you can, the girl replied with a further slip in both respect and formal language, *but you and im,* she

added emphatically, inclining her head towards John *may ave to stand if there aint no seats when you travel. And the journey takes?*

The girl smiled as though she was about to reveal some great secret. *Bout five hours if things are good. Up to ten if there is problems.* Minutes later Rachel was walking towards the train. The old stations of Kings Cross and St. Pancreas, as she vaguely remembered them, had long since been merged

into one huge complex with a few long distance coaches leaving from wasteland nearby. She had heard coach prices were lower, but one look left her with the feeling that most risked arriving in pieces. There were also rumours that they could be stuck mid-journey for days if they failed to find fuel. She had to ask the way twice to find her platform. The old platform numbers had been covered over at some point, but some of the covers had been ripped off by scavengers looking for re-sellable materials; the result was a hotchpotch of confusing directions and numbering.

To John's disappointment, and her horror, the train was only a slight improvement on the local commuter she had used a year of so earlier. The entire structure shook violently when the engine started, though a young trooper who sat next to John assured them that the engine was a new one using the latest bio-fuel technology and they would be *Ok* for their journey. As they bumped off, it occurred to Rachel that the carriages might not be capable of dealing with the speed of a new engine, but her concerns faded as they set off at little more than a crawl, out of the station complex and through the first cuttings and tunnels. Emerging again into sunlight, the trooper pointed out the work under way to rebuild what he said was *The Old Emrates Stadium.* She felt certain that the name was wrong, but John was so excited at the spectacle, and so certain that *My Dad will take me there when he comes back from abroad*, that she remained silent. She noticed though that *'abroad'* seemed to provoke a change in behaviour on the part of the trooper and, looking again at her tickets, she realized that they were sitting in the wrong part of the train having settled in second rather than first class.. But John was happy and well entertained, and the trooper was going to TyneWall, so she decided it was perhaps best to stay where they were. Looking out was depressing. The track was frequently lined with abandoned or burnt-out buildings, so Rachel took an old Realbook from her bag. It was one of her father's, but one she had never read and this was an opportunity. An example of reading might, hopefully, encourage John to get away from the electronics, though she noted the trooper's immediate disdain.

Don't worry, that's where the line separates from the old one, he volunteered as the carriage suddenly lurched violently to the left. Almost immediately she could feel both a change in the quality in the ride and a constant, gentle climb. Because of geography, the northern Wall was relatively low, but even so the line had no choice but to rise to cross it. On the far side she understood that there was a rapid descent before the line swung north westwards and thereafter, she gathered, it would cling to high ground whenever possible. She searched her memory for the term she had learnt at school to describe for the direct distance between places. *As the crow flies* eventually appeared from the recesses of her memory, though this journey was more like ...and she looked for something appropriate. *More like 'As the water doesn't flow.'* she concluded.

Chapter XIV
Aftermath
Washington Wall
May 17th

If it hadn't been for the rain and grey skies, President Lopez would have enjoyed the view from the repaired Oval Office. That said, the air conditioning was still out of order and Lopez found the combination of high humidity and 35 centigrade a less than comfortable combination. His staff had put huge effort into ensuring that The White House was repaired and returned to pristine condition as rapidly as possible, and he had raised no objections to a large chunk of the budget being dedicated to restoring this icon of Federal government.

The news in the reports on his desk was also not all bad. The loss of over half of Torgut's Atlantic Fleet and severe damage to much of the remnant had initially been a bitter blow. Smith appeared to have seriously miscalculated the trajectory of '*his unholy tsunami*' as it was being almost universally called, having swept in a more northerly direction than seemed intended. Having broken over parts of the English and Irish coasts it had obliterated almost all life crashing ashore on Iceland and Greenland. The Canadians too had suffered badly. Though much reduced, the ocean had torn through HalifaxWall and across the flat lands towards Montreal and Quebec before petering out. Though it had reached neither city, vast tracts of land had been left saline and rendered unusable. Elsewhere, in the Prince Rupert and Atlantic provinces, the few survivors owed their lives to height above sea level and building quality. The remnants of the Polar ice cap had been smashed into smaller, floating islands which were now drifting into both the Atlantic and Pacific, further disrupting the remnants of trans-oceanic transport.

But both Smith and himself had mis-calculated or mis-understood some aspect of the American psyche. In the following weeks, as news had spread of Smith's initial plan, morale amongst his supporters and troops in the south and mid-west had crumpled. He had, unwittingly, gone just that step too far. *Perhaps, if he had been successful, it would have been justified by divine acceptance or divine will or similar gibberish* Lopez had observed many times. As it was, *divine will* had served to save America. The good news for Lopez was that the attack had galvanized both his own troops and the Canadians in an astonishing manner. Federal-Canadian co-operation against the Christians had been poor, the Polar War leaving considerable bitterness on both sides. Now, both fought with a new ferocity, borne in part of fear that an undefeated Christian military would try to inflict further horrors. Under a unified command for the first time, the combined Federal and Canadian forces had broken out of their enclaves in the north and east in a first, co-ordinated attack. In some areas the Christian militias and armies had buckled and then surrendered in the face of the onslaught. Where they had resisted, they had been slaughtered without mercy.

Sheffield Safelands

29 degrees centigrade

13.22 UTC May 17th

Rachel and her newly-acquired sister-in-law sat in the front room looking out at the rain. They had got on well, these two new relatives, and John had enjoyed the freedom of the space offered by the open country. But she should be back in London.

She would have been back in London if it had not been for the rain and storms which had started with renewed violence the week after they heard of the *Crazy Christian Man,* as the media described Smith. It had become increasingly difficult to use either line down to LondonWall as section after section had been washed away, and finally the service had been suspended *Until Further Notice.* Subsequently, much to Rachel's astonishment, there had then been some publicity suggesting that coach services were

still running smoothly and seats were available for those desperate to travel. This possible route back to London had been party abandoned when she discovered that seats were directly linked to what she deemed *desperate prices. Some gov minister must have bought shares in them*,
Lucy had observed with acidic certainty. The idea had been fully abandoned when a coach was swept into a new – hitherto unnamed- river with the loss of all on board.
Lucy's biting hostility to much of political and social life hid a much softer aspect to her character, and it had taken Rachel some time to identify her deep religiosity. If she had been more observant she would have noticed the crosses scattered through the house, and with hindsight she realized that some of her comments had been less than diplomatic by way of thanks to a family which had taken her in and fed her. William, Lucy's husband, was an enormous, muscular man, standing over two metres tall. He had taken even more time to fathom- a man with an apparent endless number of roles and jobs. His passion in life – apart from an obvious one for his wife and family- was carpentry; a sad choice for any person given the critical shortage of quality timber. However, beyond being a skilled carpenter his mastery of most aspects of

construction provided him with an extensive range of contacts including with the main, local hospital's staff who were fighting a constant battle to ensure the building's integrity. This symbiotic relationship rapidly proved invaluable as John was once again ill and needed real, quality antibiotics. Within days she had learnt which products could be acquired for days spent repairing a leaking roof or patching a wall, and given the intensity and frequency of the storms she understood why Lucy's house was so well provided.

Though she knew she should be back in London, she had also come to realize that little would be served by being there. There was no news of Henry, though the European military had informed London that the wreckage of *'his'* dirigible had been found crashed in some God forsaken marsh somewhere in southern Spain or Portugal - they seemed very vague on which- but that no bodies had been found. The assumption was that the crew had bailed out and would be trying to make their way to safety, but no more information was forthcoming.

More search flights? she had questioned. *No fuel* had come the reply.

From Henry's colleagues she gathered that the entire southern European defence system was in a state of maximum alert following the interception of messages from Caliphate forces speaking of a Christian invasion force cutting across the Atlas Mountains. There was, she had been informed with a sort of matter-of-fact sadness, no prospect of the European diverting further resources in the search of a few individuals. *You need to prepare for the worst*, had been the final, well-intentioned, advice.

Washington Wall

10.08 UTC May 27th

Lopez had vowed to abandon religion totally after his wife's death, murder as he termed it, but now he was praying. Yet again, the rain lashed mutely on the armoured Oval Office windows, the drops thrashing the pond which had formed outside and threatening to pour into the newly re-built anti-aircraft emplacements. The document in front of him ran to only two pages, and was hedged with scientific caveats of the *may*, *could*, *possibly*, *probably* varieties. The conclusion was also a *hypothetically*, but informed him *with a high level of probability* that Smith had enjoyed at least a partial victory. It was hard to find climatologists these days, many having been killed in the anti-scientific populism before and during The Religious Wars, but the few who could be located, and their latest modelling, *suggested* that Smith's destruction of the last of the Polar ice, and what *appeared to be* some modifications in Atlantic

Ocean currents were the explanation for the continued poor weather. *The data suggests, with a high level of probability, that unusually high temperatures and rainfall amounts will continue into the foreseeable future. Other areas, by contrast, may experience short periods of unusually cold weather. Harvests are likely to be negatively impacted and flooding a great risk.* he read again. *Oh shit!* he screamed to the astonishment of the assistant waiting for his response to the document. *Get me a double whiskey.*

Haifa Military Complex
13.13 UTC May 27th

It was still unclear exactly what had gone wrong with the initial plan. The immediate impact on Monroe's fleet of the waters surging into the Mediterranean had been the loss of nearly ten percent of his vessels. Many claimed that the bombs had been detonated when the tail of the fleet was still too close and that ships had been overwhelmed by the combined blast and mountainous waves. Monroe was the first to admit that things had not gone well, but argued that he had been left with no choice because of the enemy warship. Smith was also prepared, reluctantly, to admit that things had not gone to plan, though initially he gloated over the loss of Wuccie lives in the north. His own pet project had also been a failure. A reconnaissance expedition back to The Straits found the width had been reduced, but the waters were still navigable by small warships in single file. This information had cost two of the three vessels sent on the mission- the Europeans were proving difficult neighbours. Further bad news came in information from spies across the Christian Confederation which revealed Smith's disciples to be in disarray. To The President's horror, his forces had not reacted positively to attempt to obliterate what he insisted were the filthy WUCCIE scum, and were either surrendering or being defeated in the field. Monroe had read of one of the German leaders at the end of one of the major wars who had been in a bunker in a place called Berlin and was ordering his armies into battle long after they had been annihilated. The scant information he obtained suggested that Smith was engaged in desperate attempts by short-wave radio to contact generals and majors who were already in a Federal prison or mouldering in a grave. Smith had, of course, to find a scapegoat. Initially, and much to Monroe's surprise, he had gone for Adams. Smith had immediately stripped him of his rank, and so Lieutenant Adams would be the one to blame for the failure of the President's plan. There had been some contact with Adams and the pitiful– some privately said *'heroic'*- remnants of his command. He had last been heard from somewhere in the Atlas Mountains, a small matter of local resistance being greater than expected it appeared. But there had been no time to discuss what had occurred and caused their plans to fail.

Deprived of this first scapegoat, and doubtless with some assistance from Tuckman, Monroe had become the physical manifestation –the necessary *sacrificial lamb* he had been reminded-to face a military board. *Yes*, he had physically touched The President without permission, but *assault* was not appropriate nor was *attempted assassination. Yes* he had exploded the nuclear devices without The President's authority, *but he could explain this – if anyone dared or wanted to listen.* Some did, and Monroe realised that the initial focus on Adams might have been a reflection of Smith's concern about trying Monroe. There had been a relatively major mutiny when the news had been announced, though Tuckman's skill in ensuring control over weapons had given his men a distinct, ultimately crucial, advantage.

From where Monroe stood the whiteness of the deep snow lying across the landscape bore witness to the new world which their efforts had created. It was something of a mystery, the previous day being so unbearably hot, but then the hand of the Lord always seemed to move in a mysterious manner.

Much had been learnt from intercepting the frenzied European communications as the ocean surge created by the explosion had surged along the coast. No one had been able to predict its path with success, and several major European Walls had been overwhelmed before the tsunami had moved further north and westwards. There had been an immediate, furious, response from the European military which had destroyed a significant part of his fleet before they had reached the protection of their Brothers in the eastern Mediterranean. Both he and Smith had been much surprised by this, European military capability having greatly improved since the previous conflicts.

What had clearly gone wrong with the plan had been the impact on the weather. Unstable for years, the claim now was that the Atlantic currents had been diverted – temporarily or permanently was unknown- by *Adam's bomb*s and that the current unseasonal weather was the result. Some of the intelligence being gleaned from the WUCCIE scientists contained claimed that the closure of the Mediterranean in itself had been enough. It was true that this had not been agreed with the Brothers in New Eden, and during the trial they had been blamed for changing the weather and so threatening their precious, carefully developed, agricultural systems.

Despite their substantial losses, Monroe's fleet – or Smith's fleet depending on opinions- would have been sufficiently powerful to have bent The Brothers to their will. Deep splits existed between the various groups in relation to their management of relations with the outside world, and the arrival of several hundred vessels crammed with military capacity was not without implications for the balance of power. What had deeply disappointed Monroe was his own failure to predict events. True, he had never trusted Tuckman and had shared a widespread belief that he manipulated Smith as his eminence grise. But then he had never considered the possibility of his being able to use the Presidential Guard and a small number of marine units to launch a coup against both Smith and himself. There had been resistance, but with both the key leadership figures isolated and under arrest, this had been crushed. If nothing else, the Christian Confederation had taught compliance to those who appeared to be in power – being in power naturally implied they had The Lord with them.

Smith's reaction had been less disappointing because more predictable. The President had,

Monroe now clearly understood, been unstable to varying extents for years – though this had been disguised as his communicating directly and intimately with The Lord. Within hours of his arrest he had been reduced to a whimpering wreck, and had proved useless during the trial in either defending himself or assisting in the defence of others. Not, if Monroe were honest with himself, that this would have made any difference. The trial was of the 'show' type – for treason against somebody or something apparently - which Smith had perfected and in which both Monroe and Tuckman – with relatively greater and smaller levels of regret – had participated. Now, at this time, Smith stood next to him, sobbing uncontrollably.

Monroe shivered in the unseasonal cold. He was obliged to admire the way things had been organized. As sea levels had risen, the original port at Haifa had been expanded by cutting back into the valley which lay behind. In so doing, a naturally protected harbour had been created with the city – later town- perched on the slopes down to it and the ridges offering perfect emplacement for military hardware. With the exception of those which had been severely damaged and needed urgent repairs, the Christian ships were anchored at the entrance to the harbour complex, and had been especially drawn up today in a magnificent crescent facing the harbour entrance. From where he stood on *Genesis,* he could see the entire fleet clearly. It reminded Monroe of a painting he had once seen – was it the Turkish attacking the Venetians or something of that ilk?- though in that picture there had been lots of gold and Latin commentary, and certainly no snow. He was still trying to remember the name of the picture when Tuckman gave the signal for the gallows doors to fly open.

CadizWall

May 27th

Marie-Claire and Henry sat together against the trunk of a stunted tree, while the remainder of the crew lay partly concealed in a shallow ditch to their right. Covering the distance between their crash site and here had been an interminable nightmare, the marshes full of marauding groups which would have gladly killed them for a single item of clothing. *Clothing* was an interesting term, though the general consensus was that some remained beneath the filth they had accumulated. From a distance it might have appeared that the tree's base was actually encircled by an intermittent ring of blue (air force uniforms) and brown – which Henry had unwisely termed '*marsh uniform*'. The joke had failed.

And now they had arrived ......where? There was a near-unanimous conviction that they had successfully made their way to CadizWall, there was nothing else in the region which had survived and equalled it in size, but there was no written confirmation and this place was but a shadow of what they had been expecting. Greater certainty was given to their conviction by the sight of the giant cranes which had once, so Marie-Claire assured them, served what had been the naval dockyards. These now lay toppled, their latticed booms frequently sticking into the water like the beaks of their avian name-sakes. From their vantage point it was impossible to establish if the Walls had been damaged by one of the waves or if they had simply fallen into a state of disrepair amidst the regular Atlantic storms. The Wall immediately in front of them had itself been substantially breached, revealing the streets of the old city which rose steeply towards the hill which formed the core of the settlement. There was at least some element of hope in that. 'We take the risk?' Marie-Claire demanded. The question was democratic and extended to both her crew and Henry.

Personally, I would rather die than continue to live on what you call survival rations, Henry replied immediately with considerable conviction. He had visibly lost weight and developed a rudimentary beard which, though she found it hard to acknowledge given the circumstance, Marie-Claire found profoundly attractive.

Careful English, growled one of what had been the gunners. *You left your rations onboard, so we been feeding you. Not too late die,* and she touched her sidearm while smiling slightly. Minutes later they were, once again, wading through water towards the Wall. The consensus had been that death through starvation or disease awaited them outside, and that they might encounter either assistance or a quicker death within.

Eight months later
Sheffield SafeLands

Draped in a thick cover, Rachel sat in an old armchair nursing her new daughter. The arms were worn thin with use, but there was a re-assuring softness to the fabric - redolent of a time when things had been easier- and it seemed the chair was becoming hers through traditional use. This new status was almost confirmed when Lucy mentioned that it had been her mother's when they lived on the Humber marshes. The chair always sat in the large bay window overlooking the hills which rolled southwards towards what had been Sheffield. On the horizon, the sky was darkening once again, the massing black clouds ripped jagged with lightning and bringing yet another prematurely early night. As always, it was raining. The thick clouds shrouded the sun so effectively that it already seemed to be late on a December day.

The pregnancy had not proved to be an easy one. It had proved even more difficult than usual to get access to the hospital this time – even Will's skills appeared to be increasingly redundant as talk turned more and more to the threatening shortage of food if the rains did not end soon. Eventually, he had bribed a technician who had done the scan and a range of tests in the depth of the night in exchange for promises of future work.

A movement in the distance interrupted her thoughts and she watched absently as a military vehicle crawled up the remnants of the road which led past the house, its path marked by the trail of smoke belching from it. It had to be military, the red light in the front a clear warning to other road users to clear the way, and she assumed it was on its way to the communications tower further up the hill. Then, to her surprise, it suddenly swung across the road and up the drive leading to her new home, the wheels spitting a cloud of gravel behind the vehicle before it slid to a halt in front of the door. The engine was immediate turned off to save fuel and there were several minutes of silence apart from the pattering of the rain. Curious, she sat watching and heard the dull thud of an armoured door closing on the vehicle's far side. Seconds later an emaciated, but familiar, figure walked slowly through the beams of the headlights towards their front door.

At the Time of the Presidents' Wars:

Between Hell and High Water

Chapter I

WashingtonWall January 23rd.

Three Days After the Re-established Presidential Inauguration Ceremony

President Lopez had started the day a happy man. The November elections had been run in what was generally considered to have been a fair, democratic manner. Even the former Christian Confederation states had been allowed, and encouraged, to vote. The turn-out in those areas had been low, but produced a very slim majority in his favour. The weather had also- a rarity- started well, though by mid-morning the usual patterns of heavy rain and stifling humidity had re-established themselves. *Smith may not have drowned us* Lopez often commented in meetings *but over time the weird weather he created is doing just that.*

Then the less- than- good news had started to arrive. The first had been that Federal forces had been halted in their assault on one of the last remaining Christian Confederation strongholds in the Carolinas. It had not been a defeat, but -after the relative ease with which the enemy's forces had been decimated in the north and mid-west- Lopez felt deeply the loss of yet more lives amongst the Federal troops he commanded. The extremely bad news was now sitting in front of him in the Oval Office.

Ed Fitzpatrick had been the president's Chief Scientific Officer for nearly a year now, though this was the first one-to-one meeting between the two men. Fitzpatrick's was a dangerous post, the prior incumbent having been assassinated by Christian Confederation agents and the previous two office holders having resigned soon after having received their first death threats. The meeting had started with a good cup of RealCoffee, though after reading Fitzpatrick's report Lopez had already decided that a glass of something very strong would be needed by the end of the meeting. *So, let me understand this correctly*, he demanded. *What you are saying is that the destruction of the ice sheets caused by Smith's explosion has changed things yet again? I thought that we had already seen all the changes caused by the environmental mess we made earlier, and expected that now things were going to settle down.* Fitzpatrick took a long sip of his precious RealCoffee before leaning forward in his chair and looking Lopez directly in the eyes. *Mr. President, with all respect we submitted our first report on this in May of last year. I remember you being really upset about it at the time, but you have had other things to deal with- not least trying to finish the war. We've had more time, and a few more resources, to look at this more closely and, as we wrote earlier, Smith seems to have changed –or perhaps accelerated – the old climatic order in the Atlantic.* His original tone had communicated the frustration he felt, but the sentence ended with a distinct quiver in his voice. *The explosions caused a change. We don't understand how or why exactly, but there was some real skill involved in those explosions – blocking a 300 metre deep channel took some doing and certainly changed the shape of both Spain and North Africa. Shame we don't have any* satellite shots.

Lopez raised his hand to stop Fitzpatrick's flow. *So that was enough to cause all of this?*

Fitzpatrick hesitated, taking another sip before continuing. *Perhaps. The initial tsunami destroyed much of what remained of the Arctic ice, and that appears to have had huge implications. Then again there will have been some changes in sea salinity…*

Sea Salinity? How does that fit? Lopez halted him again.

Salinity changes density, changes currents. The Med was salty, so perhaps that did something to the Atlantic. We cannot be certain, we simply don't have the resources to monitor the ocean as we used to do, but what we are seeing – and he waved his hand in the direction of the windows in the Oval Office- *are weather patterns which fit very closely with some very good academic work from before*

The Troubles. Some of what is happening seems to be pretty basic, predictable stuff.
Changes in ocean temperature change oxygen absorption, acidity and a range of other factors. And, one other issue – those explosions seem to have caused a minute shift in our inclination towards the sun. Only minute, but….well perhaps enough a make a permanent difference.
Ah God! Lopez declared, burying his face in his hands. *Do you have any good news?*
Fitzpatrick smiled grimly. *I'm not a betting man, but whatever Smith did will almost certainly have changed the climate in the Med. So whatever remained of his fleet may not be very welcome.*

Printed in Great Britain
by Amazon

60232665R00180